Pra
THE BEAST AI

"Delightful from the first sentence, reminiscent of Roald Dahl and Neil Gaiman at their cleverest."
—SLJ

"Meggitt-Phillips's ability to make readers squeal with delight, squirm in discomfort, and squawk with laughter make classical comparisons inevitable. . . . Bound to whet appetites."
—Kirkus Reviews

"I loved it! (Was that okay, Jack? Please don't feed me to the beast!)"
—James Riley, *New York Times* bestselling author of Story Thieves

Also by Jack Meggitt-Phillips

Revenge of the Beast

The BEAST and the BETHANY

By Jack Meggitt–Phillips
Illustrated by Isabelle Follath

ALADDIN

NEW YORK LONDON TORONTO SYDNEY NEW DELHI

ALADDIN

An imprint of Simon & Schuster Children's Publishing Division

1230 Avenue of the Americas, New York, New York 10020

First Aladdin paperback edition December 2021

Text copyright © 2020 by Jack Meggitt-Phillips

Illustrations copyright © 2020 by Isabelle Follath

Originally published in Great Britain in 2020 by Egmont UK Limited

Also available in an Aladdin hardcover edition.

All rights reserved, including the right of reproduction in whole or in part in any form.

ALADDIN and related logo are registered trademarks of Simon & Schuster, Inc.

For information about special discounts for bulk purchases, please contact

Simon & Schuster Special Sales at 1-866-506-1949 or business@simonandschuster.com.

The Simon & Schuster Speakers Bureau can bring authors to your live event. For more information or to book an event contact the Simon & Schuster Speakers Bureau at 1-866-248-3049 or visit our website at www.simonspeakers.com.

Book designed by Heather Palisi

The text of this book was set in Goudy Old Style.

Manufactured in the United States of America 1121 OFF

2 4 6 8 10 9 7 5 3 1

The Library of Congress has cataloged the hardcover edition as follows:

Names: Meggitt-Phillips, Jack, author. | Follath, Isabelle, illustrator.

Title: The beast and the Bethany / by Jack Meggitt-Phillips ; illustrated by Isabelle Follath.

Description: New York : Aladdin, 2020. | Series: The beast and the Bethany ; [1] |

Summary: Handsome Ebenezer Tweezer has lived comfortably for nearly 512 years by feeding the magical beast in his mansion's attic whatever it wants, but when the beast demands a child, they are not prepared for Bethany.

Identifiers: LCCN 2020033454 (print) | LCCN 2020033455 (ebook) |

ISBN 9781534478893 (hardcover) | ISBN 9781534478916 (ebook)

Subjects: CYAC: Monsters—Fiction. | Beauty, Personal—Fiction. |

Wealth—Fiction. | Orphans—Fiction. | Behavior—Fiction. | Humorous stories.

Classification: LCC PZ7.1.M46775 Be 2020 (print) | LCC PZ7.1.M46775 (ebook) |

DDC [Fic]—dc23

LC record available at https://lccn.loc.gov/2020033454

LC ebook record available at https://lccn.loc.gov/2020033455

ISBN 9781534478909 (pbk)

For Maureen Meggitt, a 511-year-old who
almost certainly keeps a beast in her attic
—J. M.-P.

For Amy, my wonderful agent
—I. F.

The Purple Parrot

E benezer Tweezer was a terrible man with a wonderful life. He never went hungry because all his fridges were piled with food. He never struggled to understand long words, like confibularity or pinickleruff, because he very rarely read books.

There were no children or friends in his life, so he was never troubled by unpleasant noises or unwanted conversations. There were also no parties or celebrations for him to attend, so he was never hot and bothered about what he should wear.

Ebenezer Tweezer didn't even have to worry about death. At the time this story begins, he was within a week of his 512th birthday, and yet, if you were to have bumped into him on the street, you would have thought him to be a young man—certainly no more than twenty years old.

You might also have thought that he was quite handsome. He had short golden hair, a small nose, a soft mouth, and a pair of eyes which dazzled like diamonds in the moonlight. There was also a wonderful look of innocence about him.

Sadly, looks can be deceiving. You see, at the time when this story begins, Ebenezer was about to do a very bad thing.

All Ebenezer did at first was walk into a bird shop. He then patiently waited behind an impatient person at the till. The impatient person was a small, bony girl who was wearing a backpack with two stickers on it. One read BETHANY and the other BOG OFF!

"I wanna pet!" said the girl to the large, pleasant bird-keeper.

"What sort were you looking for?" he asked in return.

"A frog! Or a panther! Ooh, or a polar bear!"

"'Fraid you're in the wrong place. The polar bear and panther shop is down the road, and the frog market is only open on Wednesdays. We can do you a bird, but not much else," explained the bird-keeper.

The girl reached into her backpack and pulled out a flip-flop, a half-eaten cookie, two seashells, and a ruler that

said PROPERTY OF GEOFFREY on it. She laid out all the items on the counter.

"What kind of bird will that buy me?" asked the girl.

The bird-keeper looked thoughtfully at the items and did some sums in his head. "If you give me the backpack as well, I'll give you ten worms," he said.

The girl was very pleased with this offer. She shrugged off the backpack and handed it over. In return, the bird-keeper took out ten worms from his pocket and plopped them into her hands. The girl barged past Ebenezer and out of the shop.

"Sorry 'bout that, Mr. Tweezer," said the bird-keeper. "How can I help?"

"That's quite all right," said Ebenezer. "I've come to pick up the Wintlorian purple-breasted parrot."

When the bird-keeper brought out the sleeping parrot, Ebenezer did not snatch it away. He waited for the cage to be handed over, and he stayed in the shop to speak for a while even though he was not a big fan of conversation.

"This is a special one, remember now," said the bird-keeper. "Only twenty of them left in the world. You ain't the sorta person to lose him, are you?"

"I won't do that," answered Ebenezer, shuffling where he stood.

"You don't get many of these around no more—took me a long time to track one down. Ain't every shop can get you a real talking, singing parrot. Especially ones that sing proper human songs, instead of those tweety ones. These sorts of birds love an audience. You ain't that sorta person what's gonna keep it for yourself, hidden away, are you?" asked the bird-keeper.

"I won't do that," said Ebenezer. He was feeling most uncomfortable under the bird-keeper's gaze.

"These sortsa birds need a lotta care and attention. They need love. You ain't gonna treat it bad, are you?" asked the bird-keeper.

"Of course not!" answered Ebenezer, in a high and shaky voice.

The bird-keeper knew and loved each one of his birds, from the aquatic warblers to the yellow-legged seagulls, and he did not want to see any of them go to a bad home. He took a long, hard stare at Ebenezer.

"I know exactly what sorta person you are," said the bird-keeper, after a second or two of staring.

Ebenezer gulped.

"You're a great bird owner!" said the bird-keeper. "I can see it in your face!"

Ebenezer smiled with relief and handed over the money. He paid far more than the agreed price, as a special thank you to the bird-keeper for his hard work.

He bid farewell and left with the caged and sleeping parrot. He climbed into his car and started the short drive back to his house. Just as he was parking, the parrot woke up with a large yawn.

"Good morning!" said the parrot, in a distinctly unparroty voice. He spoke in low, chocolatey tones.

"It's late afternoon," said Ebenezer.

"Whoopsie-poopsie! Well. Good late-afternoon. My name is Patrick."

"And mine is Mr. Tweezer. Welcome to your new home."

"Whoa and gosh!" exclaimed Patrick.

The "whoa" and the "gosh" were both the right sorts of words to say, because Ebenezer's house was nothing short of extraordinary. It was fifteen stories tall and twelve elephants wide. The front of it had been painted red, and the gardens were large enough to host a dozen different tea parties, all at once.

As Patrick looked up from his cage, he was filled with excitement. He was a well-traveled parrot, having performed singing tours in several countries, but he had never seen anything like this. He wanted to fly around every part of the house and take it all in.

"Can I come out of my cage now?" he asked.

"Not yet," answered Ebenezer. "There's someone I want you to meet first. Well, some*thing* is perhaps a better description."

Ebenezer got out of the car and took Patrick into the house. He headed up the stairs, carrying Patrick in his cage.

"This thing lives on the top floor," said Ebenezer. "And it's very excited to meet you."

Ebenezer climbed the stairs, while Patrick took in everything around him. The journey up fifteen flights of stairs passed quickly, as Patrick looked around at all the beautiful pictures and antiques that lined the walls.

"Try not to be scared," said Ebenezer, once they reached the top floor. "It won't like you if you are scared."

Ebenezer pushed down the handle of the rickety old door at the top of the stairs. It opened with a creak.

He switched on the light. The room was not like the rest of the house at all. It was damp and smelled strongly of boiled cabbage. It was bare, save for the presence of a set of red velvet curtains and a small, golden bell at the end of the room.

Ebenezer walked over to the curtains. He paused before drawing them open.

"Don't shout and don't scream. It doesn't like those sorts of noises," he warned Patrick.

Ebenezer drew the curtains open and revealed the beast. The beast was a big blob of gray, with three black eyes, two black tongues, and a large, dribbling mouth. It had tiny hands and tiny feet.

Ebenezer was pleased to see that Patrick reacted remarkably well. He didn't scream and he didn't shout, *Ewww, gross!*

After taking a moment to compose himself, Patrick said, "Good morning! My name's Patrick."

"It's late afternoon." The beast's voice was soft and slithery—like a snake made of feathers. "I want you to sing."

"What would you like me to sing?" asked Patrick.

"Sing a song about me!" demanded the beast.

Patrick paused for a moment. Then, he began to sing.

"The beast has the finest house in the land.
It's so tall and long and terribly grand.
Even the Queen, with her palace so wide,
Couldn't compete with the beast if she tried."

Ebenezer was impressed. The tune was pleasing to hear, and the lyrics seemed to make the beast happy.

"The beast has a face, so useful and round.
With three eyes to make sure lost things are found,
And two tongues for licking all it can find,
The beast is quite clearly one of a kind."

Patrick stopped singing. He said he was sorry that it was such a short song, and that he would be able to sing something a little longer once he got to know the beast better.

Ebenezer let out a sigh of relief when he saw that the beast was smiling. The smile was wet with dribble.

"That was beautiful. Tell me, are there many birdies like you?" asked the beast.

"Oh gosh no. There are only twenty of us left in the whole world." Patrick's eyes filled with purple tears. He tried to distract himself from his own sadness by asking, "How many beasts like you are there?"

"I am the only one, the last survivor." The beast smiled as it said this. "It's good that you're rare. I like rare things. Come a little closer so that I can see you better, birdy."

The beast eyed Ebenezer expectantly. Ebenezer picked up the cage and brought Patrick closer to the beast's three black, blinking eyes.

"Closer," ordered the beast.

Ebenezer dragged the cage so that it was within three footsteps of the beast.

"Even closer," said the beast.

Ebenezer brought the cage so that it was right in front of the beast's large, dribbling mouth. The smell of boiled cabbage was now eye-wateringly strong.

"Can you see me now?" asked Patrick, a little nervously.

"Oh, I could see you fine the whole time," said the beast, as it licked its dribbling mouth with its two black tongues.

"Then . . . then why did you need me to come closer?" asked Patrick.

It was the last question that he ever asked.

The Unusual Request

A wonderful life can turn someone into a terrible person. It makes you forget that there are people in the world who have problems, and this can stop you from really caring or worrying about others.

So you can understand how Ebenezer Tweezer came to be one of the most selfish men who ever lived. After spending nearly 512 years without difficulty, Ebenezer had never really learned about pain or sadness.

He found it impossible to imagine what these things must feel like, and so he didn't feel guilty about feeding Patrick to the beast. He thought it was a shame that he would never hear Patrick sing another song, but he didn't waste any time thinking about how horrid it must have been for the poor little parrot.

Instead, Ebenezer went downstairs—all fifteen flights of them. He opened one of his many fridges and began to make himself a beef and mustard sandwich.

The bread was made with the finest seeds, taken from the very tops of the Himalayan mountains. The beef and the butter came from Dolly, a charming Welsh cow who had won World's Loveliest Udders for three years on the trot. Meanwhile, the mustard had been made using expensive white wine and rare black truffles.

It promised to be a delicious sandwich. However, before Ebenezer could take a bite, the beast rang its bell. Reluctantly, Ebenezer set down his sandwich and made the journey back upstairs.

The beast was waiting in the damp, cabbagey room. It was humming a song to itself—the same song that Patrick had sung.

As Ebenezer walked in, the beast let out another happy burp. A shower of purple feathers came floating out with it.

"Good evening," said Ebenezer, offering a polite nod.

"And good evening, Ebenezer! What a very fine evening it is, don't you think?" asked the beast.

Ebenezer was thinking about his sandwich, and about how much he was looking forward to eating it. He hadn't given much thought to the evening and whether or not it was a fine one.

"I said it's a very fine evening, Ebenezer," said the beast in its slithery voice. "Do you agree with me?"

"Oh yes, it's a very mustardy evening," answered Ebenezer.

"Mustardy! What do you mean by mustardy?!"

"Sorry, I don't know what came over me. I didn't mean to say mustardy, what I meant to say was . . . was . . ."

"It doesn't matter, Ebenezer," said the beast crossly. "All that matters is that it's a very fine evening. Very fine indeed!"

"Yes, of course."

The room was silent for a moment. Ebenezer was too hungry to think of anything to say, while the beast was deciding whether it wanted to be in a good mood or not. After a moment or two, the decision was made.

"Oh, I can't stay cross with you, Ebenezer. Especially after you served me such a delicious dinner," said the beast.

"I'm glad you enjoyed it," said Ebenezer.

"It's so nice to eat something with personality," said the beast. "The rusty taste of the cage was also a nice touch."

"Sounds like a *unique* flavor," said Ebenezer.

"It really was. Now what would you like as your reward?"

This was how it worked. Ebenezer would bring the beast various things to eat, and in return the beast would provide presents. Diamond chandeliers, a witch's broom, giant stuffed teddy bears—there was no object that the beast couldn't conjure up for Ebenezer.

"I would like a piano," said Ebenezer. "And please could I have one of those baby grands—a pretty little one, which I can carry down the stairs. Ideally, one that will grow into a handsome, adult grand."

"Well, well, well, Ebenezer. I never thought I'd see the day when you would take such an interest in music. Would you like some piano-lesson books with that as well?"

"Goodness no!" said Ebenezer, disgusted by the suggestion. "I am not going to play it. I only want to put it in the front living room so the neighbors can see."

"What a strange man you are," said the beast. "But your wish is my command."

The beast closed its three black eyes and shut its dribbling mouth. It started to wiggle its blob of a body and made a low humming noise as it moved from side to side.

Then, all of a sudden, the eyes opened again. The beast stopped wiggling, stretched its mouth wide open, and vomited out a baby grand piano.

The piano was slimy with dribble, but aside from that, it was perfect. It was just the size that Ebenezer wanted, and it was definitely pretty enough to make the neighbors jealous.

"Thank you very much," said Ebenezer. He picked up the piano and marched toward the door. Then he turned around. "Oh, I almost forgot. There's something else I need from you as well."

"And what might that be?" asked the beast.

"A birthday present," answered Ebenezer. "On Saturday it'll be my 512th birthday, and I can already feel the wrinkles starting to come back on my face. I'll need another of those anti-aging potions, please."

"No problem at all, Ebenezer. I'm happy to help."

The beast closed its three eyes and started to wiggle again. But then it stopped.

"Is everything all right?" asked Ebenezer.

"Everything's superb," answered the beast. "But I've decided to ask you to do something for me, before I give you this year's potion. I want you to bring me another meal."

Ebenezer sighed. He wished he had asked for the potion before the baby grand.

"I might not be able to get you another Wintlorian purple-breasted parrot," warned Ebenezer. "There are only nineteen left in the world now."

"I don't want another one of those, so there's no need to worry," said the beast. "I already know exactly what I want. And it's something I've never tried before."

Ebenezer found this difficult to believe, because he had brought the beast all manner of things to eat. During the last month alone, the beast had feasted upon seven pearl necklaces, an antique chest of drawers, two beehives, and a medium-sized statue of Winston Churchill.

"Is it something rare?" asked Ebenezer.

"It's not rare, but it is rarely eaten," answered the beast. "It's noisy, it comes in all shapes and sizes, and it's something that can be found in every country in the world."

Ebenezer thought for a moment, struggling to think

what the noisy, common thing might be. He was never very good at figuring out the beast's clues.

"Is it some sort of trumpet?" he asked.

"It is not." The beast laughed a slithery little laugh. "I am severely allergic to trumpets. That would be the end of me."

"Is it a poodle? Do you want me to go to the dog shelter again?" suggested Ebenezer.

"No, no, no," said the beast, laughing again. "It's not an object, and it's not an animal."

Ebenezer was out of ideas. He thought that "trumpet" and "poodle" were both excellent guesses.

"Let me put you out of your misery," said the beast. "The next thing I want to eat is . . . a child."

A gleeful and dribbly smile slowly spread across the beast's face, as it watched Ebenezer come to terms with the suggestion.

"Sorry, but I think I misheard you there," said Ebenezer.

"I said I want to eat a child!" boomed the beast. "I want to know what one tastes like. I want a juicy, plump little child. I want to gobble it up in one oozy, squishy bite."

Ebenezer shifted nervously. He suspected the beast wasn't finished yet.

It wasn't.

"I want to know what a snotty nose tastes like," it sighed dreamily. "And chubby cheeks, dirty fingernails, and nit-ridden hair!"

The beast was breathless and sweaty with excitement. It looked at Ebenezer with furious hunger and energy in its eyes. Now, in a much softer voice, it asked:

"So when do you think you might be able to bring me one?"

The Heated Conversation

Y ou can't eat a child!" said Ebenezer.

The smile dropped from the beast's face. Now, in its place, stood a nasty sort of snarl.

"And why not?" asked the beast. "You've brought me everything I've wanted before. Why are you turning your nose up at this one?"

"Because it's wrong!" said Ebenezer. "You can't go around eating children. There's something very *impolite* about it."

"Impolite? Did you say impolite?" asked the beast. "You didn't think it was impolite when you brought me a Wintlorian purple-breasted parrot, and you didn't think it impolite four hundred years ago when I asked you to bring me the last dodo."

"But that was different!" said Ebenezer. "Animals aren't the same as children."

"That's a silly way to think!" said the beast.

"No, it's not. And I'm sorry, but I just won't do it," said Ebenezer. It was the first time he had stood up to the beast in over five hundred years.

The beast gave no sign that it was disappointed. In fact, it looked almost maddeningly calm.

"If that's how you feel, Ebenezer, there's nothing I can do," said the beast. "And thank you for being so honest with me."

"Um . . . that's . . . well, that's quite all right," said Ebenezer. "Sorry I can't be more helpful."

Ebenezer walked toward the door, delighted and surprised by the fact that he had managed to say no to the beast. He was just turning the door handle, when the beast spoke again.

"Oh, by the way Ebenezer, I do hope you enjoy old age," said the beast. "I really hope you enjoy having the wrinkles on your body, and the pains in your joints as you walk up the stairs."

"What do you mean?" asked Ebenezer.

"I mean what I say," said the beast. "I mean that I hope

you are happy when old age starts weakening your bones and writing lines into your beautiful face."

"None of that will happen," says Ebenezer. "The potion will stop all of that from happening like it normally does, won't it?"

"Oh, I'm sure it would, dear boy. But where are you going to get the potion from?" asked the beast. "You're not getting it from me, unless you bring me what I want."

"But—"

"No buts," said the beast. "You need your potion by Saturday, and I want to eat a child before then. Bring one to me, and you will continue to live a long and happy life."

"And if I don't?"

"Then you shall die, Ebenezer. Without the potion, your body will give in to your old age, and you will be nothing more than a pile of bones. I would be most upset about it."

Ebenezer wondered whether he cared that much about children after all. He didn't really want to feed one to the beast, but he also didn't think that any child was worth more than his own life.

"Are you sure there's nothing else I can bring you to eat instead?" asked Ebenezer.

"A child is the only thing I want," answered the beast.

"Well, then," said Ebenezer. "Let me think about it."

The thinking didn't take very long.

"I've thought about it, and I think it's a wonderful idea. There's no reason why you shouldn't have a child to eat," said Ebenezer. "Would you mind vomiting out a large brown bag for me? Ideally the same size as the one you gave me when I went hunting in the South Pole."

The beast hummed and wiggled and vomited out a strong, emperor penguin–sized bag. Ebenezer ran downstairs and jumped into the car with it.

He drove straight to the zoo, beeping and weaving his way through the traffic with all the patience of a cranky toddler. He made it to the ticket office with just ten minutes to spare before closing time.

"Adult or child?" croaked the old lady at the ticket office. She was small and scaly, and looked like she might be better suited to the lizard enclosure.

"I want a child, please," said Ebenezer breathlessly.

The lizard lady peered closely at Ebenezer and raised her thin eyebrows in a questioning manner.

"I mean, an adult ticket. Because I am an adult," said Ebenezer quickly, as he laid down some coins. "It may surprise you to learn that I'm actually 511 years—"

The lizard lady didn't care. She snatched the money and let Ebenezer and his bag through the barrier.

But Ebenezer didn't focus on this. He was too busy congratulating himself.

He knew there would be children at the zoo, because he had spotted a few during the time he had kidnapped a peacock to feed to the beast, but he had no idea there would be so many. The place was an all-you-can-eat buffet of snot and nits and tiny fingernails.

Ebenezer approached a frowny girl who was standing

near the elephant sanctuary. He opened his large brown bag and invited her to jump inside.

"Come on then," said Ebenezer, when the girl refused to play ball. "I haven't got all day."

"DADDY! DADDY! IT'S A STRAAANGERRR!" shouted the girl.

Within moments a man (similarly frowny), marched up to Ebenezer. He shouted twelve rude words and made two nasty threats, before he led his daughter away.

Ebenezer shrugged, and then tried his bag trick on another child.

And then another.

And then another two more.

Every time he found a child, there was a blasted parent lurking somewhere nearby. Pretty much all of them had unpleasant things to say when they saw Ebenezer try to stuff their children into his bag.

Soon, the complaints mounted up, and Ebenezer was dragged back to his car by a security guard the lizard lady had brought with her. He finally accepted the fact that he would have to think of something else, when he received a lifetime ban notice from the head zookeeper.

The something else that Ebenezer thought about was a sweetshop. Whenever Ebenezer went to his local sweetshop, there were always greedy children with sticky fingers and dirty mouths swarming around the place. And some of these children were there without their parents. The only adult who could get in Ebenezer's way was the sweetshop's eccentric and experimental owner, Miss Muddle—

Mr. Ebenezer Tweezer's Candy Palace

annoyingly, all the children seemed fascinated by her.

In order to get around this problem, Ebenezer decided to set up his own sweet stall. He got the beast to vomit out a banner, which read MR. EBENEZER TWEEZER'S CANDY PALACE, and he set up a table on the street, filled with all manner of sweet goodies that he sprinkled with sleeping powder so that he could easily transport the children to the beast's attic.

After a short while, Ebenezer's first customer arrived. He was a twelve-year-old named Eduardo Barnacle, who was in possession of the world's third largest set of nostrils. They were wide enough to each hold a small orange.

"Well, well, well—what do we have here?" asked Eduardo. He bent over Ebenezer's table and took a deep sniff of each of the sweet things on offer.

"We have licorice allsorts, Catherine wheels, strawberry fancies, sherbet pips, banana bonbons—the whole party."

Eduardo sniffed again. The rims of his nostrils swelled and shrank greedily upon his nose.

"This is the strongest selection I've seen in a while. Congratulations, Mr. Tweezer," said Eduardo. He was oddly confident in his ability to speak to grown-ups as if he were one. "How much will it cost if I purchase a sample of each one?"

"Two hundred and fifty-three pounds and sixty-two pence," answered Ebenezer, a little too quickly. He wasn't used to dealing with money, because he normally relied on the beast, so he didn't really know how much things cost.

Eduardo shook his nostrils (and the rest of his head) sadly from side to side, and walked away from Mr. Ebenezer Tweezer's Candy Palace. Ebenezer chased after him.

"Sorry, sorry—I got that all wrong. I meant to say eighty-five pounds and ninety-four pence. What a bargain!" he said.

Still, Eduardo continued to walk away, so Ebenezer offered the sweets to him for free. Then he offered to pay Eduardo to eat them.

"How much will you give me?" asked Eduardo.

"Seven hundred and forty-six pounds?" suggested Ebenezer.

"Well, clearly your sweets can't be very good then. Good day, Mr. Tweezer."

Eduardo marched back home, with his nostrils held high in the air, and refused to return. Ebenezer resumed his position behind the table, helped himself to a Catherine wheel, and pondered whether he should remain outside. He promptly fell asleep, face-first into a strawberry fancy, before he remembered the sleeping powder.

Seven hours later, in time with the sunrise, Ebenezer sat up, somewhat chilly from his night on the street. He decided that he had had quite enough of this sweetshop business.

"There has to be an easier way!" he said crossly to himself.

For the first time in his life, Ebenezer was sad that he didn't have a family of his own. It would have saved so much time and energy if he could have just fed one of his children to the beast.

He went back to the house, changed clothes, ate some truffles on toast, and climbed into his car. He drove straight to the bird shop, where the bird-keeper was busy feeding some parakeets their breakfast.

"Good morning," said Ebenezer.

"Ah, Mr. Tweezer!" said the bird-keeper. "So happy to see you. I had an awful dream about Patrick last night. I dreamed he was screaming for my help. Ain't anything wrong with him, is there?"

"He was a bit uncomfortable last night," said Ebenezer. "But I think it was just indigestion. That's all over now, thankfully. He hasn't screamed at all today."

"Oh good, that's such a relief. I was so worried," said the bird-keeper. "So what can I do for you? Are you looking to buy a friend for the parrot?"

"In a way, yes. I'm looking for someone who will join Patrick in his new home."

"Well, I got loads of them here. I had some society finches come in last week. Would you like to see them?"

"I actually have something in mind already," said Ebenezer. "It's a bit of an unusual request. I was wondering whether you might have any children for sale?"

"Did you say 'canary'?"

"No, I said 'children.' I'm not fussy about size, and I don't really mind whether it's a boy or a girl."

"Right . . ." The bird-keeper took a quick look around his shop. "Sorry, mate, but I don't think we got any of those. Got a lovely little cockatoo, at a very reasonable price, if that works? Or a half-moon owl?"

"No, thank you, I only want a child. How about the

one who came in here yesterday? I believe her name was 'Bogoff'?"

"Never seen her before last night, I'm afraid. And hope I never see her again. The backpack turned out to be broken in several places, and that cookie was far too soggy," said the bird-keeper, shaking his head.

"I see," said Ebenezer. "I suppose I'll have to try elsewhere."

"Wait a mo," said the bird-keeper, as Ebenezer started to leave. "Why are you wanting a child?"

"It's just something I need. My life depends on it," said Ebenezer.

"Ah, how sweet. I remember my wife and I felt the same before we had little Tommy. A child is a wonderful thing," said the bird-keeper.

"This little Tommy, would you be willing to part with him? I'll pay whatever price you ask," said Ebenezer.

"He's not for sale!" said the bird-keeper. "My wife would kill me."

Well, it was worth a shot, thought Ebenezer. He started making his way toward the door again. His shoulders were slumped and he was feeling very sorry for himself.

"Oi!" said the bird-keeper. "You can't give up just like that."

"I don't really know what else I can do," said Ebenezer. "There are too many parents at the zoo."

"Eh?" The bird-keeper frowned. "Haven't you tried the orphanage?"

"The orphawhat?" asked Ebenezer. It was a word he had never heard before.

"Yeah, you should try the orphanage three streets down. Miss Fizzlewick runs it, and she's got dozens of little ones who need a home."

"But what about the parents?" asked Ebenezer.

"That's the whole point, these children ain't got no parents. The parents are dead, or lost, or just not around."

Ebenezer was surprised. He had no idea that people had such sad lives.

"Do you think I'd be able to get one by Saturday?" he asked the bird-keeper.

"Don't see why not."

"Marvelous, absolutely marvelous!" Ebenezer opened his wallet and threw a wad-load of cash at the bird-keeper to thank him for the very excellent advice. "You're a lifesaver!"

Ebenezer ran out of the shop and jumped back into his car. All he had to do now was find the orphanage.

The Children's Menu

The orphanage was a squat, ugly building with cracked windows and peeling paintwork. There was a rusty sign at the top of the gates, which read INSTITUTE FOR GENTLEMANLY BOYS AND LADYLIKE LADIES.

Ebenezer shuddered as he looked at the place, and he was shocked that anyone was expected to live there. He thought it was no wonder that the orphanage had so many children going spare. It was not the sort of place that attracted customers.

As Ebenezer got out of his car, he was met by Miss Fizzlewick, the director of the orphanage. She was a tall, thin woman, with stern eyebrows and a wild tangle of gray curls at the top of her head.

"Good morning," said Ebenezer.

INSTITUTE FOR
GENTLEMANLY BOYS
AND
LADYLIKE LADIES

Miss Fizzlewick flinched. "The correct greeting when meeting a *lady* for the first time is 'how do you do?' Now, are you bringing children, or looking to take one away?"

"Take one away, please," answered Ebenezer.

The twitchy beginnings of a smile formed at the corner of Miss Fizzlewick's lips. It had been several weeks since she had been able to get rid of a child.

"You should have said sooner. Come on through!" she said.

Miss Fizzlewick decided to show Ebenezer that she was now in a "friendly" mood by smiling at him. Her teeth were yellow and cracked, and her gums were an unhealthy shade of dark red.

"As you can see, I keep a firm watch over this place," she said, as she led him into the building. "I believe it's impossible to raise well-behaved boys and good little girls unless everything is kept clean and tidy."

Ebenezer laughed, because he thought this was a joke. The orphanage was dusty, dirty, and littered with cobwebs.

"Is there something you find funny?" she asked.

"Um, no. I was just thinking about something I saw on TV the other day," answered Ebenezer.

Miss Fizzlewick flinched again. She didn't approve of modern technology. "Watching television is most *ungentlemanly*," she said.

Miss Fizzlewick led Ebenezer into her office, which was guarded with a sign that read NO CHILDREN UNLESS ABSOLUTELY NECESSARY! The room was significantly less dirty, dusty, and cobwebby than the rest of the orphanage, and it was filled with all sorts of fabulous and beautiful things that weren't on display anywhere else.

Miss Fizzlewick took a seat at her desk. It was hidden underneath a mountain of paper and teacups.

"I'm very organized," she said with a serious face. Ebenezer didn't laugh this time. "Would you like anything to drink?"

Ebenezer was thirsty, but he didn't believe that anyone who was so unorganized would be able to make a good cup of tea.

"No, I'm fine, thanks," answered Ebenezer.

"Good, good. Now let me just fill out the paperwork," said Miss Fizzlewick. She fumbled around her desk before finally finding a blank form. "What's your name?"

"Mr. Ebenezer Tweezer."

"Do you live in the area?"

"Yes, a five-minute drive away. Three if I went fast."

"Excellent. How old are you?"

"511, but on Saturday I'll be 512."

Miss Fizzlewick looked up from the form, baffled by Ebenezer. She brushed some gray curls away from her ears and asked Ebenezer to repeat his answer.

"Thirty," said Ebenezer. "Yep, that's what I meant to say. I'm thirty years old. Gosh, I'm so young."

"Well, if you don't mind me saying, I think you look even younger than that, Mr. Tweezer. You don't look a day older than twenty," said Miss Fizzlewick, with a toady smile.

Ebenezer always felt a rush of pride when he heard this, in spite of the fact that he had been paid the compliment several times.

"Anyway, let's get on with the important business," continued Miss Fizzlewick. "What type of child are you looking for?"

"I'm not fussy," said Ebenezer. "Just give me the cheapest one you have."

"The cheapest?"

"Yes, please. But if the cheapest is total rubbish, then I'm willing to pay more."

"Mr. Tweezer, do you know how an orphanage works?"

asked Miss Fizzlewick with a suspicious frown. "You do know that you don't have to buy the children? We give them to you for free!"

Ebenezer thought this was a very odd way to run a business. Perhaps if Miss Fizzlewick charged for the children, then she might have enough money to afford a prettier building. However, he wasn't going to complain.

"Marvelous," said Ebenezer. "So what happens next?"

"Well, now you meet the children. I'll line some of them up outside my office so that you can interview them, one at a time. How old would you like the child to be?"

"I don't mind," said Ebenezer.

"How about shoe size? A lot of people are favoring children with a size four shoe these days."

"I don't mind," said Ebenezer.

"Mr. Tweezer, you must have some idea of what you're looking for. You must know whether you want a boy or a girl?"

"I really don't mind," said Ebenezer impatiently. All he could think about was getting the potion as quickly as possible. "Honestly, any child will do."

Miss Fizzlewick wished that Ebenezer had at least one opinion on the matter. It would have made the business of getting rid of a child a lot easier.

"Right then," said Miss Fizzlewick. "I guess that you're going to have to meet *all* of the children. I hope you don't have any plans for the rest of the morning."

Miss Fizzlewick went to fetch the children, all twenty-seven of them. She lined them up outside her office, while Ebenezer tapped his fingers impatiently on the desk.

"Here's the first one. Her name's Amy Clue, and she's just joined us. Come on in, Amy, and for goodness' sake, don't be shy. It's very annoying," said Miss Fizzlewick.

Amy was a shy little girl, and her shyness wasn't helped by adults telling her not to be shy. She was no older than three and not much taller than a tennis racket. She poked her head nervously around the door and looked at Ebenezer.

"How do you do?" said Ebenezer. He offered Amy a hand to shake.

After much nagging, Miss Fizzlewick dragged Amy into the room. She hugged a battered pink teddy bear in one hand and waved shyly to Ebenezer with the other.

Amy was too small to reach the chair, so Miss Fizzlewick lifted her up and let her stand on the desk. Amy smiled at Ebenezer, while Miss Fizzlewick wiped her hand on her trousers to get rid of any germs she might have picked up.

"Ewoh!" said Amy.

"I beg your pardon?" said Ebenezer.

"Ewoh!" said Amy, waving again. "Ewoh! Ewoh! Ewoh!"

Ebenezer was unsure about how he was meant to respond.

"I'm afraid she's rather behind on her elocution lessons," said Miss Fizzlewick, sighing impatiently. "She's trying to say 'hello,' AREN'T YOU, AMY, MY DEAR?"

"Oh, I see," said Ebenezer, wincing at the volume. "Ewoh to you too, Amy. It's a pleasure to meet you. Well, well, well, what do you think about the weather today? Hasn't it been miserable?"

"Eh?" asked Amy.

Miss Fizzlewick explained that Amy was still learning to speak, and that she didn't know what words like "weather" and "miserable" meant. Miss Fizzlewick told Ebenezer that he should stick to simple, toddler-friendly topics.

"Ah. Quite right." said Ebenezer.

He didn't spend much time speaking with toddlers and he found it tricky to think of what to say, but then he hit upon the brilliant idea of talking to Amy about her teddy bear.

"What's his name then?" he asked, pointing at the teddy.

"'S not a boy!" Amy laughed so hard, she looked like she might fall off the table. "'S a girl, an' is named Miss Lillipie."

"Miss Lillipie, eh? What a fun name. Good morning,

Miss Lillipie, how do you do?" asked Ebenezer, offering another handshake, but this time to the teddy bear.

Amy found this funny. The desk wobbled, as she let out a roar of laughter.

"E's funny!" said Amy, pointing at Ebenezer. "I like him."

Ebenezer liked Amy as well. She wasn't going to win any conversation prizes, and she needed to work on her annoying laugh, but aside from that, she was very cute.

"Mr. Tweezer, what do you think? Would you like to take Amy home with you today?" asked Miss Fizzlewick, as she rubbed her bony hands together.

"Yes," said Ebenezer. "Yes, I would."

Amy squealed with delight and started dancing round the table with Miss Lillipie. Miss Fizzlewick shrieked with joy, and her twitchy smile broke out into a triumphant, yellow-toothed grin.

Ebenezer was happy as well, and he thought it would be good fun to have Amy around the house—it would certainly be more enjoyable talking to her than the beast.

Ebenezer gasped, as he thought about the beast. For a moment, he had forgotten why he had come to the orphanage in the first place. He wasn't here to find a child he liked; he was here to choose a meal for his master.

"Wait, no!" blurted Ebenezer. "No, no, no—I can't take Amy! She's not what I want!"

Amy stopped dancing around the table with Miss Lillipie. She stopped squealing with delight and started crying instead. She lifted her arms for someone to cuddle.

Miss Fizzlewick huffed impatiently, dumped Amy on the floor, and ordered her to stop sniveling and sobbing all over the place. Ebenezer looked at his watch, wondering how long it was going to take. He was already a bit bored with spending time in the orphanage.

"Perhaps the next one will be more your cup of tea," said Miss Fizzlewick, as Amy left the room."

The next one was a tall, polite boy named Geoffrey. His parents had drowned in a lake two years previously, and he had been trying to honor their memory by being as good a boy as possible ever since.

As he came into the office, he lingered in front of a fabulous, glittering snow globe, featuring a ballerina dancing in the street.

"Miss Fizzlewick, is that my mother's snow globe?" he asked.

"Never mind that, it's perfectly safe here. Besides, it's most ungentlemanly to ask a lady about her private property."

"Sorry, Miss Fizzlewick—it won't happen again."

Ebenezer could already tell that Geoffrey was far too nice to feed to the beast.

"Next!" shouted Ebenezer, while Geoffrey was in the middle of introducing himself. "I don't want this one either."

Geoffrey was dragged outside by Miss Fizzlewick. Ebenezer got through another ten children within the space of twenty minutes. All the ones he saw were far too pleasant. He had no idea that it would be so tricky to find a bad child.

"I thought you weren't fussy," snapped Miss Fizzlewick. "I thought you said that any child would do."

"Yes, sorry for the delay," said Ebenezer. "But I need to be absolutely sure I get the right one."

Miss Fizzlewick was growing impatient with Ebenezer. There was a certain frostiness in her voice as she introduced the next child. "This one is called Harold Chicken. Hopefully he'll be more your cup of tea."

Ebenezer could tell almost immediately that Harold Chicken was not going to be his cup of tea. For one thing, he was too smartly dressed to be bad, and for another he was smiling with too much kindness.

Ebenezer was about to shout "Next!" when he heard a scuffle taking place outside the office. Geoffrey was screaming, "Help! Help!" and a girl was shouting, "Shut up, you little rat!"

Ebenezer leaped off his chair and joined Miss Fizzlewick to see what was happening. Geoffrey was pinned on the floor by the small, bony girl from the bird shop. The girl was shoving worms up his nostrils, and she was shouting, "Rat! Rat!" at him.

"Stop that at once, Bethany!" screeched Miss Fizzlewick.

Bethany sulked as she removed her worms and fingers from Geoffrey's nostrils. Miss Fizzlewick turned to Ebenezer.

"I'm sorry you had to see that, Mr. Tweezer," she said. "I should have left Bethany in her room."

"No need to say sorry," said Ebenezer, with a wide smile on his face. "After all, I should be saying thank you. I think you have just helped me find the child who I want to take home."

The Bethany

You want to adopt Bethany?!" asked Miss Fizzlewick.

They were back in her office. Miss Fizzlewick had sent all the children to their rooms, except Bethany, who was told to wait outside.

"Yes, please," said Ebenezer. "Is that going to be a problem?"

"It will probably turn into a problem for you," said Miss Fizzlewick, pursing her lips.

She told Ebenezer about how Bethany had arrived at the orphanage after her parents had died in a fire, and she warned him that Bethany had been nothing but trouble ever since.

Bethany had pulled every prank and trick imaginable since she had been at the orphanage. She had squirted superglue on toilet seats so that anyone who sat on one would be trapped in the bathroom for days, she had filled the sugar pot with chili powder to ruin Miss Fizzlewick's cups of tea, and she had left banana peels on every staircase, which led to nasty falls for many of the children.

Miss Fizzlewick explained that it wasn't just the naughtiness that was an issue, it was the joy that Bethany took in doing horrible things. Unlike most children, Bethany didn't show any remorse after she had been told off. She seemed to be very proud of her behavior.

"I've never met any girl so determined to be unladylike," said Miss Fizzlewick. "You'll have a battle on your hands if you take her in."

"I'm confident it's a battle I can win," said Ebenezer.

"Don't be. There was another woman like you who came here a few years ago. She thought she knew everything about children, and that she could get the better of Bethany."

"What happened to her?"

"She took Bethany home, but brought her back three days later after Bethany threw all of the woman's china dolls into the washing machine."

Ebenezer was happy to hear this. He was sure that he had finally found the perfect child to feed to the beast.

"Bethany has no manners. She never wears any of the pretty dresses that are laid out for her, and she eats her food like a barnyard animal," said Miss Fizzlewick. "I want you to think very carefully before taking her into your home."

Ebenezer thought carefully. This took all of three seconds.

"I still want Bethany," he said. "And I can promise you that I will never bring her back."

And so it was settled. Miss Fizzlewick told Bethany that she had a new home, and that she was to collect her things at once. By the time Ebenezer had finished signing all the necessary forms, Bethany was waiting outside with a box containing a catapult, a toothbrush, a whoopee cushion, a pile of clothes, a crumpled photograph, the last two worms, and a stack of comics.

There was a twinkle of mischief in Bethany's eyes as she looked at Ebenezer. She was sizing up her latest target and thinking of all the ways that she might go about tormenting him.

"Last chance, Mr. Tweezer. Are you absolutely sure about this?" asked Miss Fizzlewick, looking doubtful that Bethany wouldn't soon be back in the orphanage.

"Positive," answered Ebenezer. "Goodbye."

Ebenezer led Bethany to his car, while whistling a happy tune.

"You're a rubbish whistler. You sound like a granny trying to spit out a cough drop," said Bethany, as she climbed into the back seat.

In response, Ebenezer continued to whistle—louder and with more enthusiasm than before. He started the engine. He was just pulling out of the orphanage when he saw Geoffrey running toward the car, shouting, "Wait!", "Stop!", and "Oh, bother, please don't go!"

"Drive!" Bethany shouted at Ebenezer. "Don't just sit there, you nitwit, let's go!"

Ebenezer certainly wasn't going to follow any of Bethany's instructions. He stopped the car and rolled down the window to speak to Geoffrey.

"Thank . . . *oof* . . . you . . . *ah* . . . very . . . *eek* . . . much," said Geoffrey, who was out of breath after his run.

"Look here, you seem like a nice chap, but I'm afraid I can't take you home with me. I've already chosen to adopt Bethany, and I don't need anyone else," said Ebenezer.

"Yeah, so buzz off, you rat!" said Bethany.

"It's . . . *aaah* . . . not. . . *ow* . . . that," said Geoffrey.

He took a moment or two to catch his breath. "I'm here because Bethany took some things that belong to me. They were the last gifts I ever received from my parents."

Ebenezer raised his eyebrows at Bethany. He wasn't cross; he was just impatient to get home. Bethany frowned.

"Here you go, you rat," she said. She took the last of the worms from her box and threw them out of the window.

Ebenezer drove the car away from the orphanage.

He didn't hear Geoffrey shouting, "Not the worms, it's the comics! She's taken my comics!"

"Will anyone else come chasing after us?" Ebenezer asked Bethany.

"Nah. Only him," said Bethany. She was now sorry that she hadn't stolen from anyone else.

"Wasn't he the same person whose nostrils you were stuffing? Any particular reason you're not a fan?"

"It's because he's a rat," said Bethany.

"Right. Fair enough," said Ebenezer.

They passed the rest of the journey in silence. Bethany flicked through Geoffrey's comics, while Ebenezer looked at himself in the mirror. He noticed that there was a faint wrinkle above his right eyebrow.

"I must get my hands on that potion," he muttered to himself.

"You what?" asked Bethany.

"Never mind, it doesn't concern you. Right, here we are. Welcome to your new home!"

Bethany looked up at the fifteen-story house that was as wide as a dozen elephants. She shrugged and returned to reading the comics.

"Aren't you going to say 'Whoa!' or 'Gosh!'?" asked Ebenezer.

"Nah," said Bethany. "There's nothing impressive about a waste of space."

Ebenezer's cheeks flushed red. He was about to shout at Bethany, but then he realized that there was no point. She would be in the belly of the beast soon enough.

"Come on then, let's go inside," said Ebenezer.

"Do we have to? This car's probably comfier than that dump of a house," said Bethany.

"That dump is worth more than three castles put together!" shouted Ebenezer, unable to hold his temper any longer.

Bethany grinned, delighted that it had been so easy to make him cross. She chucked the comics back in her box and jumped out of the car.

"I want to choose my room," said Bethany, as Ebenezer walked them inside. "And I want it to be bigger than yours."

"That's fine by me," said Ebenezer. "But there's someone I want you to meet first. Well . . . some*thing* is perhaps a better description."

When Ebenezer looked at Bethany, he experienced a new feeling. For the first time in his life, Ebenezer was actually looking forward to feeding the beast.

The Moveable Feast

This thing lives on the top floor," said Ebenezer. "And it's very excited to meet you."

"If it's so excited to meet me, then why doesn't it come downstairs?" asked Bethany.

"It doesn't like to move, unless it's absolutely necessary."

Ebenezer headed up the stairs, followed reluctantly by Bethany. The journey up fifteen flights passed slowly, as Bethany made fun of all the pictures and antiques that lined the walls. Some were criticized for not having proper faces, others for not being colorful enough, and others for being just plain "boring."

By the time they reached the top of the stairs, Ebenezer was ready to push Bethany back down them. He didn't,

however, because he knew that the beast liked its meals to be fresh.

"Try not to be scared," said Ebenezer. "It won't like you if you're scared."

"If it tries anything scary, it won't like me!" said Bethany.

Ebenezer rolled his eyes. Bethany would find out soon enough that no one was a match for the beast. He creaked open the rickety old door and switched on the light. The room smelled strongly of boiled cabbage and dead parrot.

"Poo-ey!" yelled Bethany, as she shoved two bony fingers up her nose to block out the smell.

"I wouldn't say that if I were you. It doesn't like the smell to be mentioned," whispered Ebenezer. "And please don't shout or scream. Those sorts of noises are not welcome here."

"It doesn't like baths, either," said Bethany, her voice bunged up by the fingers in her nose. "Has it heard of shampoo?"

Ebenezer drew open the red velvet curtains to reveal a very unhappy-looking beast. Clearly, the curtains were not soundproof.

When Bethany caught sight of the beast, she screamed wildly. She pulled her hand out of her nose and pointed a bony, booger-covered finger at the beast.

"Eww, gross!" shouted Bethany. "That is absolutely disgusting! It's just a big old horrid lump of eyes, tongues, and gray!"

"Please don't listen to her," said Ebenezer to the beast. "She doesn't know what she's saying. There's nothing old or horrid about you—you're a majestic lump!"

The beast turned its three eyes to Ebenezer. None of them looked happy.

"I mean, you're not a lump at all. Of course you're not a lump," blurted Ebenezer. "What I meant to say is that you're . . . you're . . ."

"I'm hungry," said the beast.

"Yes, exactly! You're hungry!" said Ebenezer.

The beast returned its eyes to Bethany. The look it gave her was not a friendly one.

"You're a very rude child. Tell me, are all children so very rude?" asked the beast.

"No idea. I don't know all the children in the world. What about beasts? Are they all slimy and ugly?" asked Bethany.

Ebenezer felt that he had seen quite enough of Bethany for one lifetime and that it was about time she was shut up. He had no idea how that other lady who adopted her had managed to last for three days.

"Would you like Bethany to come closer to you, so that you can see her better?" Ebenezer asked the beast.

"I'm not going one step closer to that thing, until it learns how to use a toothbrush!" said Bethany. "Its breath smells worse than a bag of rabbit poo!"

"Bethany, I don't care what you think. You must learn

to follow instructions, and if the beast wants you to come closer then—"

"I don't want her to come closer," interrupted the beast. "I can see her just fine from here. And frankly, I've seen enough of her already."

"Awesome!" said Bethany. She ran out of the room and back down the stairs just as fast as her legs could carry her.

Ebenezer was so shocked by the beast's behavior that he didn't even try and stop her. He was amazed and appalled that it had gone off its dinner so quickly.

He looked to the beast for an explanation. But it didn't seem inclined to give one. Its three eyes stared stonily at the door Bethany had just cheerfully departed through.

Ebenezer didn't ask it any questions, in case it was still cross, so the room was silent, save for the distant sounds of Bethany stomping through the house and slamming doors.

"I'm very disappointed in you, Ebenezer," said the beast eventually. "For centuries, you have never failed me. When I asked for a leopard, you scoured the jungle for the best you could find. When I asked for the remains of the

Titanic, you bought a snorkel and went deep-sea diving. But now, when I ask you for something so simple, you fail me."

"I know, I know, and I'm sorry," said Ebenezer. "I made a mistake with Bethany. She's such a horrible little girl, and I should never have brought her to you."

The beast looked puzzled.

"Her horridness has nothing to do with my disappointment. In fact, the bad behavior might give her an interesting, bitter flavor," explained the beast.

It was Ebenezer's turn to look puzzled. He stared with openmouthed confusion at the beast.

"Oh, Ebenezer, do I have to explain everything to you? Come on, have a think. What did I tell you that I wanted to eat?" asked the beast.

"You . . . well, you said you wanted a child, didn't you?"

"Ah, but not just any child. I said I wanted a *juicy, plump* child! I want one with lots of flesh that I can sink my teeth into, not this little thing that you've brought me. When I eat my first child, I want it to feel like a meal, not a snack, and I want to chew on more than just a sack of bones."

"Oh, right, now I get it," said Ebenezer. He showed how much he was getting it by nodding his head and clapping his hands together. "It's simple! I'll take back Bethany and ask Miss Fizzlewick if she has any brats in a larger size."

"NO!" boomed the beast, wobbling angrily. "THAT'S NOT WHAT I WANT!"

Ebenezer waited for the wobbling to stop.

"What *do* you want?" he asked in his softest and most soothing of voices.

"I want to eat Bethany! I want to gobble her up and show her how scary a slimy lump of gray can be. But I don't want to do it until there's more of her to eat," answered the beast.

"When will there be more of her to eat?" asked Ebenezer.

"After you've fed her piles of food, you fool! Today is Tuesday, yes?" Ebenezer answered with a nod. "Well, you don't need your potion until Saturday. Three days is plenty of time to fatten up a child."

Ebenezer was horrified by the thought of having to live with Bethany for three days. At that moment in time, he would have happily chopped off his own ankles if it could have saved him from spending any more time with her.

"But, please—" said Ebenezer.

"No buts, Ebenezer," said the beast. "If you disappoint me again, then I'm afraid that you won't find me so generous with my gifts."

The Big Feed

For one of the first times in his life, Ebenezer had a problem. And it was a big one.

The big problem was that Bethany was not big enough. If he wanted to keep living his charmed, wrinkle-free life, then he had to find a way of putting meat on her bones as quickly as possible.

As Ebenezer walked down the stairs, he wondered whether there was a way of getting rid of Bethany by the end of the day. He thought of a few ideas, but none of them were really winners.

His first thought was that he should sneak into the hospital, steal some needles, and inject several packages of chocolate cookies into Bethany. It looked like it was going to be a solid plan, right up until the moment Ebenezer remembered that he was squeamish around any sort of medical equipment.

His next idea also looked like it was going to be a smasher. In order to avoid having to spend three days with Bethany, Ebenezer decided that he would try and trick the beast. He would get Bethany to wear several layers of clothes—at least seven sweaters and three and a half pairs of trousers—and then present her to the beast, claiming that she was now the right size to eat.

Upon closer inspection, however, there were two clear problems with this plan. First of all, Ebenezer would struggle to persuade Bethany to wear seven sweaters and three and a half pairs of trousers. And even if he did succeed in getting her to wear such a ridiculous outfit, he would find it impossible to persuade the beast, after the event, that a child could taste so much like a pile of clothes. The beast would probably get cross, and vomit fire and hammers at him.

Ebenezer's third idea came to him while he was standing on the eleventh floor. He paused for a moment to look at the pieces of art that lined the walls.

The eleventh floor was home to some of Ebenezer's favorite paintings. It contained the picture of the lady with her nose put on backward, and the one of the married couple who didn't look very happy to see each other. On the wall farthest away from the staircase, there was also the one with the skeleton head that was smoking a cigarette.

Ebenezer didn't know a lot about art, and he didn't really care much for the paintings themselves. He liked them because he knew that each one meant a lot to other people. With the help of the beast, and its ability to vomit out piles of money, Ebenezer had managed to beat dozens of other gallery and museum owners to make sure that these paintings belonged to him and no one else. It made him happy to think that he owned something that everyone else wanted.

Even though Ebenezer was no great fan of art, there was one picture on the eleventh floor that he really liked. It was a small, book-sized portrait called *The Golden Boy*.

The picture always brought joy to Ebenezer. And now it brought him an idea.

As he stood in front of the golden boy, Ebenezer was struck by his third, and most sensible, solution to the Bethany problem. He decided that it was time to be patient.

The golden boy, with his happy smile and sparkling eyes, seemed to be telling Ebenezer that it was all going to be all right. He seemed to be saying, *Don't worry, you handsome devil, you can last three days with this wretched child.*

Ebenezer nodded in agreement with the picture. "Yes," he said. "Yes, I am a handsome devil, and yes, I can do it! After all, what's three days in the life of a 511-year-old anyway?"

Ebenezer continued his descent, now far happier than he was before. As he made his way down the remaining flights of stairs, he saw that Bethany had been into every bedroom she could find and had made a mess in each one. She had defeathered pillows, she had crumpled bedsheets, she had thrown clothes out of wardrobes and cupboards, she had left muddy shoe marks on the carpets, and she had even pushed over the odd item of furniture.

Ebenezer should have been trembling with fury, but he wasn't. The memory of the golden boy calmed him, and let him shrug off the mess as if it were nothing more than a speck of dirt.

He strolled into the kitchen to find Bethany waiting for him at the dining table, with a grin on her face. She was happy to see him—it offered her a new opportunity to make mischief.

"You finished with Stinky Breath then?" she asked.

"Soon, Stinky Breath will be finished with you," he mumbled.

"Eh?" She paused to pick her nose. "Anyway, I'm hungry!"

"So is Stinky Breath."

"Well, shut up and cook us some grub then."

Ebenezer considered chucking Bethany in the oven, roasting her for forty-five to fifty minutes, and then serving her in a bowl for the beast. Instead, he decided to remain patient.

For "grub," Ebenezer served eight slices of cold roast beef and a turnip soufflé. Bethany picked up the plate and threw it against the wall.

"No!" she shouted. "Not that."

She shouted the same thing when Ebenezer brought her out cannelloni, a lobster jacket potato, and a bowl of cauliflower dumplings. In order to save himself from any further embarrassment, Ebenezer asked Bethany to give him a clue about what she wanted to eat.

"Chocolate cake! And ice cream! And caramel toffee sauce!"

Bethany smiled and waited to be told she couldn't eat such unhealthy things, but Ebenezer didn't show any crossness at all. He simply opened one of the dessert fridges and brought out everything that she wanted.

Bethany was disappointed. She had been looking

forward to making Ebenezer angry. She tried again.

"I want a big slice. Massive, actually," demanded Bethany.

"Fine by me," said Ebenezer.

Ebenezer's relaxed attitude irritated Bethany. She wolfed down the first slice of cake and demanded another one.

"This time I want it to be even bigger," she added.

And so Ebenezer cut another slice—an even bigger one. He served it with a larger dollop of vanilla ice cream, and squirted a more substantial squirt of caramel toffee sauce on top. This made Bethany suspicious.

"I know what you're doing—you're trying to trick me," she said, after she finished her second slice. "You're trying to make me think that you don't care. Well, it won't work! I'm not going to let you win, and I'm never ever gonna stop wanting cake! Gimme another one!"

Ebenezer cut her another one. It quickly disappeared down Bethany's throat.

"Another one!"

Ebenezer cut another one.

"And another one!"

Ebenezer cut another one.

"And another one!"

"Hold on, I'll have to fetch more cake," said Ebenezer.

Ebenezer was thrilled that Bethany was eating so much food because it made his job a lot easier. At this rate, she would be the size of a small cottage by midnight.

Sadly for Ebenezer, Bethany's stomach made a noise, and the noise it made was not a happy one. It was the sort of noise that a stomach makes after it's been forced to digest a whole chocolate cake within the space of five minutes.

The noise was a high-pitched, whiny groan. It was as if Bethany's stomach was screaming at her to stop.

"No, like literally, actually no!" shouted Bethany, as Ebenezer started to cut a fresh slice from the new cake. "Please no!"

"I thought you said that you were never going to stop eating cake?" asked Ebenezer.

He finished cutting the slice. He plopped half a tub of ice cream next to it and squirted the rest of the toffee sauce on top.

"You're not going to let me win, are you?" he asked.

In response to the challenge, Bethany picked up her cake fork. With a shaking hand she helped herself to a forkful and lifted it up to her face. She frowned with concentration as she tried to open her mouth.

"Come on then, get on with it," said Ebenezer, after a few seconds. "Or are you going to admit defeat already?"

Bethany screwed her eyes shut and shoved the cake in her mouth. The cake, oozing with sickly sweetness, slithered slowly down her throat and into her stomach.

"Owww!" said Bethany. She clutched her stomach as it made another high-pitched groan. "I can't do it, I can't eat anymore."

Ebenezer didn't know how to feel. He was disappointed that Bethany had stopped eating; however, he was also delighted to have beaten her at something.

"You're a weakling," he said to her. "I'm going to leave the cake here so you remember how pathetic you are."

Ebenezer walked out of the kitchen, put on his third-best coat, and headed toward the door.

"What are you doing?!" Bethany shouted after him.

"Going to the movies. There's a new superhero one out."

"I like movies," she said.

"Do you? How interesting. It's a shame that I don't go to the movies with weaklings."

Ebenezer slammed the door on his way out. It felt good to give Bethany a taste of her own medicine.

The Missing Cake

The movie was a boring one, filled with various flying people who kept shouting at each other. Ebenezer was also irritated by the people in front of him who laughed loudly at every bad joke that the flying people made.

He was feeling grumpy when he came back into the house, but his mood soon perked up when he noticed that there was no sign of Bethany. Clearly, she had put herself to bed.

Ebenezer's mood was further improved when he noticed that all the cake had disappeared from the kitchen. He was delighted by the thought that Bethany had eaten it all. Surely, if she had eaten two whole chocolate cakes, then she would be big enough for the beast to eat?

Ebenezer couldn't contain his curiosity. He had to see Bethany and find out what she looked like.

He jumped up the stairs, taking two at a time, and headed to the eighth floor—this was where the biggest bedroom in the house was, and it was almost certainly going to be the one that Bethany had chosen for herself. Ebenezer took a peek in the room and found Bethany lying like a starfish on the bed. She was snoring, and her fingers were covered in cake.

Ebenezer crept into the room to take a closer look. He was disappointed by what he found.

Bethany didn't look any bigger than she had been before he went to the movies. It was also very strange—there was lots of chocolate cake on her hands, but there were hardly any signs of it around her mouth. He wondered how this had happened.

On the bedside table, Bethany had laid out the crumpled photograph from her box. It was a black-and-white, faded image of a man with a mustache and a woman without any mustache whatsoever. They were sat on a pebbled beach. The man was carrying a scowling baby in his arms, while the woman held a large newspaper in hers.

Ebenezer returned the photograph to the table and

crept back out of the room. His bedroom was located on the fourteenth floor, so he headed upstairs.

As he was walking, he noticed that there was something strange about the pictures and antiques that lined the walls. He stopped to take a closer look at one and gasped in horror.

"Oh no, no, no!" he said, as he realized why there was so much chocolate on Bethany's fingers, and yet none around her mouth.

It was because Bethany hadn't eaten the second cake. She had used it to doodle over all of Ebenezer's paintings and antiques. Ebenezer ran up to the eleventh floor to see what she had done to his favorites.

It was worse than he had expected. Bethany had smeared a pair of chocolate-icing spectacles onto the woman with the backward nose, and she had drawn ice-cream smiles onto the faces of the married couple so that they now looked quite happy to see each other. She had also given a crazy caramel-toffee-sauce hairdo to the cigarette-smoking skeleton.

Ebenezer ran over to his precious picture of the golden boy. He fell to his knees.

"No! What has she done to you?!" he sobbed.

Bethany had turned the golden boy's hair black by

smearing cake into the picture. She had also added a caramel-toffee-sauce mustache to his lips, so that he now looked ridiculous, instead of beautiful.

Underneath the picture, spelled out in chocolate capital letters, Bethany had left a message:

DEAR EBENEZER

YOU SHOULD HAVE TAKEN ME TO THE MOVIES

LOTS OF LOVE WEAKLING

Ebenezer stormed upstairs, with hot tears burning in his eyes. He barged open the attic door and was surprised to find that the beast was not in its usual position.

The beast was waddling from one end of the room to the other. It was moving slowly, with great effort, and thick, syrupy beads of sweat were pouring off its body. Ebenezer rushed over to help, asking, "What's the matter?"

"Everything's FINE!" said the beast, even though it was clear that everything was not fine. It was out of breath, and its three eyes were spinning with exhaustion. "I'm exercising!"

The beast never usually exercised, and normally made a point of moving as little as possible. Ebenezer wondered why there had been a sudden change in its behavior.

"Is it because Bethany called you a blob?" asked Ebenezer.

"It's got nothing to do with that," said the beast crossly. It sat down in the middle of the room and let out a relieved groan. "Why are you here?"

"I'm here because I can't stand Bethany anymore!" said Ebenezer. "She's ruined all my pictures and antiques. There isn't a single one left that hasn't been destroyed by cake!"

The beast yawned. Its three eyes were drooping with exhaustion and boredom.

"Please, please will you just eat her before she does anything else?" asked Ebenezer.

The beast perked up. Its eyes were now wide open with interest.

"You should have said that she was ready before, old boy. Do you mean to say that she is now big enough for me to eat?"

Ebenezer looked at his feet. "She is a *little* bit bigger . . . ," he began.

"Tell the truth, Ebenezer—is there enough meat on her bones?"

"Probably not. Oh, but I can't bear it any longer. Do you know what she did to my picture of the golden boy?"

"No, and I'm sorry, but I just don't care," said the beast. "Frankly, you're annoying me again. I give you eternal youth and everything that your heart desires, and all I ask in return is for you to babysit and feed a small girl for me. If you can't keep control over one little child, it's not my problem."

"But all those paintings and antiques—they're ruined!"

The beast sighed. It closed its three black eyes and shut its dribbling mouth. It wiggled its blob of a body, while making a low humming sound. Then, all of a sudden, it opened its mouth and vomited out a variety of cleaning utensils.

On the floor, ever so slightly covered with dribble, there were mops, sponges, bottles of cleaning liquid, and one of those tiny cleaning brushes that look like broken toothbrushes. Ebenezer bent down and scooped them all up in his arms.

"Thank you!" he said, making his way toward the door. "Thank you so much!"

"Oh, and Ebenezer, do let me know if you need any

help when it comes to controlling Bethany. Your constant moaning is beginning to try my patience. I'd hate to be in a bad mood with you—there's no telling what I might do," said the beast.

✦ ✦ ✦

Ebenezer used every utensil the beast had vomited at him—the mops, sponges, cleaning liquid, and each teeny tiny brush to try and save his favorite pictures from a chocolatey death. With great patience, he managed to remove the spectacles and hairdo from the skeleton and the lady with the backward nose, and he fixed the picture of the married couple to make sure that they were once again unhappy to see each other.

Finally, he worked on the picture of the golden boy. He spent much more time, and much more attention, fixing this one. After an hour of careful cleaning, the golden boy was back to being beautiful.

Ebenezer decided that he would start cleaning the rest of the paintings and antiques after Bethany was in the belly of the beast—there was no point in doing it while she was still in the house to do more nasty things to them.

After such a lot of cleaning, Ebenezer was tired. He crawled into bed and put his head on to the pillow. It made a farting sound.

"What on earth?"

Ebenezer sat up and looked at the pillow suspiciously. He lay down on it, and it farted again. He reached a hand underneath the pillow and found Bethany's whoopee cushion.

"That's it!" he shouted to the empty room. He squeezed the whoopee cushion angrily and it farted once more. "I have to find a way to control her."

The Cunning Plan

A good night's sleep can do wonders for the brain. It can help sharpen your thinking, and if you are lucky, it can bring you answers to the most troublesome questions.

Ebenezer was very lucky on that Wednesday morning, because he woke up with a solution to the Bethany problem. The solution was a clever one, and it made Ebenezer smile as he thought about it.

"Yes! That will do the trick!" he said.

He was excited, and he wanted to show it by jumping out of bed. However, for some reason, his body was working a little slower than usual. The bones in his legs were aching, and it took him almost twice as long as it normally did to reach the bathroom.

When he got there, he peered into the mirror and shrieked. There were wrinkles around his eyes, and his hair had lost some of its color. The potion was wearing off.

"I must get rid of that child," said Ebenezer to his reflection.

Ebenezer brushed his teeth, made use of the toilet, and soaked in his morning bubble bath. Then he got dressed and went downstairs. He laid out a mountain of food for Bethany on the breakfast table, and then, to make sure she ate it, he put a sign on the table that read, DO NOT EAT!

He returned to his room and pretended to be asleep. About an hour later, Bethany woke up and stomped downstairs while screaming an annoying song at the top of her voice. Ebenezer heard her chuckle with glee when she saw the food and the sign on the breakfast table.

Ebenezer waited for exactly thirty minutes before returning to the kitchen. When he got there, Bethany was eating her fourth pain aux raisins, while reading one of Geoffrey's comics. There were three empty bowls of porridge next to her.

"Oh no! What have you done?" asked Ebenezer, with the very best horrified face he could manage in the face of such a triumph. He was trying his hardest to pretend that he was cross with Bethany.

"Breakfasted," she answered.

"Oh, what a shame," lied Ebenezer. "I wanted us to have breakfast together so that I could take some time to tell you all about the beast's magical powers."

"I thought you wouldn't want to have breakfast with a weakling." Bethany paused for a moment and lifted her head out of the comic. "What do you mean magical powers?"

Ebenezer had to stop himself from saying, *Whoopee!* at this point. He couldn't believe how well his plan was going.

"Never mind, I'll tell you another time. It won't work now anyway—you've already ruined it," he said.

"No, tell me now!" shouted Bethany. She banged one of her fists on the breakfast table, causing the jug of orange juice to wobble.

"All right, all right, calm down," said Ebenezer. "All I wanted to tell you was that the beast has magical powers and that—"

"Is the magical power having really bad breath?" asked Bethany.

"No, and I won't tell you anything else if you interrupt me."

Bethany pretended to zip her lips to show Ebenezer that she wasn't going to speak again.

"Thank you. Here's how it works," said Ebenezer. "The beast can conjure up anything in its stomach. You simply ask it for something, then it wobbles and hums, and boom—it vomits out whatever you ask for."

Bethany pretended to unzip her mouth. "I don't believe you," she said. "Magical beasts don't exist."

"Ah, but they do, and there's one in this house. Do you see that baby grand piano by the window? Well, that came from the beast."

Bethany stood up and marched over to the piano. She played "Humpty Dumpty" and "Twinkle, Twinkle, Little Star" to make sure that it worked.

"And have you seen that big television on the wall in the downstairs sitting room? The beast gave me that last month."

Bethany walked into the downstairs sitting room. She

watched five minutes of a cartoon to make sure that there was nothing wrong with it.

She walked back into the room and peered at Ebenezer in a suspicious manner. She still didn't know whether to believe him.

"So you can ask the beast for anything in the world?" she asked.

"That's right," he answered.

"Absolutely anything?"

"Uh-huh."

"Then why on earth did you ask him for a television and a tiny piano?"

Ebenezer laughed. It was a good question.

"I asked for the piano to annoy the neighbors, and I got the huge TV so that I would never have to read books," he answered. "But I've asked for much more interesting things from it before."

"What's the most interesting thing you've got from it?"

"A canoe, probably. Or maybe that invisibility raincoat."

"Oh, so it can give you magical things as well? That sounds *very* believable."

"It doesn't matter whether it's believable or not," said

Ebenezer crossly. "It's the truth! Look at my face. Does it look old to you?"

"Your eyes are a bit wrinkly," answered Bethany.

Ebenezer winced. "Never mind that. What I'm trying to say is that it doesn't look like the face of someone who's about to turn 512. I look wonderful for my age, and that's thanks to a magic potion that the beast gives me every year."

Bethany sat at the breakfast table and helped herself to another pastry. She frowned with concentration as she chewed and tried to make sense of everything that Ebenezer was telling her. It was a good two minutes before she asked him another question.

"Why?" she eventually asked.

"Why what?" he asked back.

"Why does the beast do it? Why does it just give people what they want?"

Now was the time for Ebenezer to lie. In order for his plan to work, Bethany had to believe everything that he was saying.

"Well, you see, the beast doesn't just do it for anyone. And there's a reason why I wanted to talk to you about this at the beginning of the day," he began, in his most believable voice. "The beast only performs magic for people who are well behaved from the moment they wake up," said Ebenezer. "There's nothing the beast likes more than rewarding people for their good behavior. It will give anything to someone who has been good for a *whole* day."

Bethany leaned forward in her chair. Her mouth dropped open in horror, causing a half-chewed piece of pastry to fall to the floor. "It has to be *all* day? It can't be like for an hour or something?"

"That's right. It has to be *all* day. "

"Oh poo. Well, there's no point in me starting today then, because I've already been naughty. Now where did I leave my catapult?"

"Wait a moment, just wait!" said Ebenezer. "Actually, thinking about it, I believe it might still be all right. If you're well behaved for the rest of the day, then I might be able to persuade the beast to give you what you want."

Bethany paused to think again. She picked the half-chewed piece of pastry from the floor and plopped it in her mouth.

"And the beast can definitely bring me *anything* I want?" asked Bethany. There was a surprising amount of hopefulness in her voice.

"Yes, absolutely," answered Ebenezer.

"All right then, Ebenezer. For one day in my life, I will be good!" declared Bethany. After three seconds, she frowned again. "Can you show me how that works?"

Ebenezer tried his best to explain what it meant to be good. He told Bethany that if she wanted to get something from the beast, then she had to stop playing pranks and making mischief in the house. He told her that she could start being good by cleaning the cake off all the paintings and antiques she had tried to ruin.

Ebenezer had hoped his plan would work, but he had never expected that it would prove such a success. Bethany cleaned every painting and antique within the space of three hours, and then she ate two bowls of broccoli, after Ebenezer told her that she had to eat lots of food in order to be good.

Bethany clearly wanted something from the beast, otherwise she would never have been so well behaved. Ebenezer soon become curious to know what it was, so he took her upstairs.

"I thought you said I had to be good for the whole day," said Bethany. "Will the beast give me what I want after just a few hours?"

"Yes, I'm sure it will, because you've been so very well behaved," answered Ebenezer.

"Hahaha, what a sucker," she said.

Ebenezer stopped for a break on the ninth floor. The journey up the fifteen flights was trickier, now that the potion was wearing off. His knees felt a bit creaky and he was quite out of breath.

"What's wrong with you?" asked Bethany. "And why do there seem to be even more wrinkles around your eyes?"

"Never mind those," snapped Ebenezer. "Tell me, what do you want from the beast?"

"Okay," said Bethany. "But only if you promise not to tell anyone."

"I double-triple-pinky promise," said Ebenezer.

"All right, let me whisper it to you."

Ebenezer bent down and leaned his ear to Bethany. She took a deep breath and blew a raspberry into his ear. "None of your business," she said.

Ebenezer took a deep breath before continuing up the staircase. Once he and Bethany reached the top floor, Ebenezer told her to wait.

87

"I'll be one moment," he said. "I just need to go and tell the beast about your good behavior."

Ebenezer stepped through the rickety old door, while Bethany waited impatiently outside. He woke the sleeping beast by poking its belly.

"Oh, what now, Ebenezer?" it asked. It had been having a great dream about eating some tarantulas.

"You know how you said you would help me control Bethany?" asked Ebenezer.

"Did I really say that? How stupid of me."

"Yes, you did, and it would really help me if you could give Bethany whatever she asks for. I've managed to convince her to be good, but it'll only work if you pretend that you're rewarding her for her behavior."

"I think you've mistaken me for some sort of performing monkey, Ebenezer!" The beast licked its lips as it thought how much it enjoyed eating performing monkeys. "Look, I'm not some sort of genie who grants children's wishes."

"Oh, I know that," said Ebenezer. "And I'm so sorry to ask, but it would really help me. It's so much easier for me to feed Bethany when she's trying to be well behaved."

"Fine. Let her in," said the beast, far from pleased.

Bethany came into the room. The smell was worse

than she remembered, and she had to try very hard not to say anything rude.

"I hear you've been a good little girl. Is this true?" asked the beast, studying Bethany carefully to see what weight had been gained.

"Oh yes, I've been good for nearly four hours. I hear you can do magic—is this true?" asked Bethany.

By way of a response, the beast wiggled and hummed. It then vomited out a top hat and a collection of handker-chiefs. It burped out a toy magic wand, a few moments later.

"Wow!" said Bethany. "That's so cool! My puke looks nothing like that!"

"Enough chitchat," said the beast. "What do you want from me?"

Bethany took an anxious stroll around the room. She fiddled with her sweater and chewed on her thumb. Ebenezer wondered what was making her so nervous.

"So you can give me whatever I want? Absolutely any-thing?" she asked the beast.

"Pretty much. But you know this already. Come on, just tell me what you want."

Bethany stood still. She took a deep breath. She closed her eyes while she made her request.

"I would like . . . my parents," she said.

"What?!" asked Ebenezer from the corner of the room.

"Stay out of it. This is none of your business," Bethany snapped. She turned back to the beast, sounding hopeful. "Would you be able to bring back my parents for me? Apparently, they both died in a fire." The beast smiled when it heard this. Its three eyes sparkled with joy.

"Hang on a minute, Bethany," said Ebenezer. "I'm sorry, I should have told you before, the beast can't—"

"Hush hush, Ebenezer!" snapped the beast. "The young girl is quite right—you need to stay out of her business."

"Does that mean you can do it?" asked Bethany. "Can you help me?"

"Of course I can!" said the beast.

"Look, this isn't funny," said Ebenezer. "I really think you should stop this right now. Now let's—"

Ebenezer was shushed by Bethany and the beast. They both told him off for being a nuisance.

"Now Bethany," began the beast. "If this is going to work, then I'm going to need you to tell me what your mummy and daddy looked like."

"Mum was a man with big ears and a mustache, and Dad was tall and blond," she said, quickly and excitedly.

Then she took a moment to think about what she'd said. "No, sorry, it was the other way around. Dad was mustached and big-eared, Mum was tall and not."

"Excellent. Now what about their personalities? Were your parents kind and nice, or cruel and nasty?"

"Definitely kind and nice! I hear that they were the kindest, nicest . . ." Bethany stopped speaking because there was a lump in her throat. She brushed away a pair of hot tears from her eyes. "Can you really bring them back?"

"Absolutely," answered the beast. "Come and stand a little closer and hold open your arms ready."

Bethany ran toward the beast. She held her arms open.

The beast closed its three black eyes and shut its mouth. It wiggled and hummed, filling the whole room with the sound of its voice. Then, all of a sudden, the eyes opened again. It opened its mouth and vomited an enormous puff of smoke.

Bethany dropped her arms, coughing and spluttering as she was surrounded by the black cloud. She wiped away the soot from her teary eyes and looked up at the beast in confusion.

"Oh. My mistake, there was nothing there but the smoke from the fire," said the beast, laughing in her face.

Bethany didn't enjoy the joke. She left the room without saying a word.

"That was horrible!" said Ebenezer, after she left. He didn't like Bethany, but he certainly didn't think she deserved to be tricked liked that.

"It was necessary, my dear boy," said the beast. "That girl won't be in the mood for any mischief or pranks for a very long time."

"But I didn't want you to do that! I wanted you to reward her for being well behaved!"

"Ebenezer, I told you that I would help you control her. I never said that I would be nice about it." The beast yawned. "Now leave me alone. I want to finish my sleep."

The Apology

The beast was right. Bethany was in no mood for mischief. After she'd changed clothes and cleaned the soot from her face, she sat downstairs and stared sadly into thin air. She didn't even have enough energy to watch television.

When Ebenezer saw this, he experienced a strange and unfamiliar feeling. At first he thought he was having stomach issues, so he filled up several hot-water bottles and strapped them to his waist, and then, when this didn't work, he presumed that it must be a headache. He fetched an ice pack from one of the freezers and bandaged it to his head.

It wasn't until the ice pack had melted and the hot-water bottles had cooled that he realized that something else was wrong. No matter what he did, he couldn't get rid of this unpleasant gnawing at the pit of his stomach, and he couldn't shake his feelings of discomfort.

It took Ebenezer a few more minutes before he realized that he was feeling guilty about what had happened. He knew that he should be happy, and he knew that he probably ought to thank the beast for helping him to control Bethany. However, for some reason, it didn't feel right. There was even a part of him that wished Bethany would start pulling pranks again.

Bethany deserved some sort of an apology. The beast wasn't going to give her one, so Ebenezer decided that he would have to do it himself.

He went upstairs and changed into a blue shirt and a pair of gentle beige trousers, because he felt that this was exactly the sort of outfit that one should wear to say sorry. When he came back downstairs, he found Bethany waiting for him by the front door. She was wearing her coat and carrying the box of things she had brought with her from the orphanage.

"Ah, Bethany, so glad you're up and about. I need to say something to you," said Ebenezer.

"I want to say I'm sorry," said Bethany.

This was a bit of a shock for Ebenezer. He felt that he

might have to change into a different outfit in order to deal with this conversation.

"I beg your pardon, did you say that *you* wanted to apologize?"

"Yes. But not to you. Can you drive me to the orphanage?"

Ebenezer was too surprised to make a fuss. He didn't think to ask any questions until they were both in the car.

"Why have you brought your box?" he asked, putting on his seat belt.

"Because it's part of my apology," she answered, not putting on hers. "Be quiet, I need to practice. I've never done one before."

Ebenezer drove while Bethany practiced quietly to herself. After a short drive, they arrived at the orphanage.

Miss Fizzlewick was coming to the end of her daily "ladylike smiles" lesson. She had lined up all the girls in the playground and was forcing them to stretch fake smiles across their faces.

"Come on, Amy, you can do better! No one's going to love you with a face like that," said Miss Fizzlewick.

"But my face is hurtsing," said Amy, as she clung tighter to Miss Lillipie, the teddy bear.

"That's no excuse, pain is a necessary part of becoming a lady! I want you all to go back to your rooms, stare in the mirror, and continue practicing. You're not allowed to stop until your gums bleed," said Miss Fizzlewick.

She ushered the children into the main building, and as the last one went in, she turned around to find Ebenezer and Bethany walking up the drive.

She trotted out her best fake smile for Ebenezer (the sight was far from pleasant). She tutted at Bethany.

"I wish I could say I was surprised to find you here again. What did you do this time, Bethany?" sighed Miss Fizzlewick.

"She didn't do anything," said Ebenezer.

Of course, this wasn't true, but he felt that there was no need to bring up Bethany's naughtiness. She had already been punished quite enough by the beast.

"Nothing?" asked Miss Fizzlewick. "No china dolls in washing machines?"

"None at all," he answered.

"And no bottoms glued to toilet seats?"

"I am happy to say that my bottom has been entirely glue-free. Bethany has been very well behaved," said Ebenezer.

Bethany frowned at Ebenezer, confused about why he was lying. Miss Fizzlewick was also looking confusedly at him.

"We're here because Bethany wants to say sorry," explained Ebenezer.

Miss Fizzlewick looked like she might faint. She went a bit cross-eyed, and her knees wobbled. "Is this some sort of trick?" she snapped, once she regained her balance.

"Nah. That would be a rubbish trick," said Bethany.

"This is simply wonderful news!" said Miss Fizzlewick. "But of course, I'm not surprised. Didn't I always tell you that those lessons on how to be a lady would pay off one day? Now let me know when you're ready to begin. And remember, ladylike apologies always begin with a little curtsy—"

Bethany didn't begin with a little curtsy. She scowled instead.

"I'm not here to apologize to you," said Bethany. "I'm here to see Geoffrey."

Bethany almost knocked Miss Fizzlewick over with her box as she barged into the building. Ebenezer helped Miss Fizzlewick get back on her feet.

"Extraordinary," said Miss Fizzlewick.

"Thank you," said Ebenezer, thinking that she was complimenting his blue shirt and gentle beige trousers. "I put the outfit together myself."

"Sorry, I wasn't talking about that—although you do look most gentlemanly. I mean it's extraordinary about Bethany. Unbelievable, in fact. She must be playing some sort of prank."

"Well, I'm not sure about that."

"I am. I've tried for years to get her to behave like a lady. She's one of those children who are incapable of change. And I can tell it's been a stressful time for you. Look at those wrinkles around your eyes."

"Can we PLEASE not talk about those!" said Ebenezer.

The conversation came to a halt. Ebenezer thought Miss Fizzlewick might return to the building and get on with her work, but she showed no sign of leaving.

"Do you think Bethany will be long?" he asked, shifting from one foot to the other awkwardly, like someone in dire need of peeing. He could feel his body getting older with every minute that passed.

"Oh yes, I would think so. She's played a lot of very mean pranks on Geoffrey since she's been here. If she's serious about this apology, I wouldn't be surprised if it takes several hours for her to—"

Miss Fizzlewick was interrupted by Bethany's return. Bethany stormed out of the building and toward the car. She was no longer carrying her box.

"Done!" she shouted. "Let's go!"

Ebenezer bid goodbye to Miss Fizzlewick and ran after Bethany. And as the potion wore off, he found it surprisingly hard to keep up with her.

+ + +

"How was that?" asked Ebenezer, when they were back in the car.

"Eurgh. Not as much fun as I thought it would be," she answered.

"Why did you think it would be fun?"

"'Cause everyone told me it would be. Everyone's always telling me to say sorry—they all said I'd feel *soooo* much happier if I was good."

"And you don't feel any happier?"

"Not a bit. If anything, I feel worse. Now I don't have any comics to read, or any catapults to fire."

"I can understand why you gave him his comics back, but why did you give him your catapult?" he asked.

"I told him to use it against anyone who tried to steal his comics. I tried to show him how it works, but he wasn't very good. Stupid rat."

Bethany rolled down her window. Then she rolled it back up again. And then down again, and then up again.

Ebenezer found it extremely irritating. "Could you stop that, please?" he asked.

"Yeah, I could," answered Bethany.

But she didn't. She rolled it up and down and up and down and up and down and . . . well, then she got bored, and stopped.

"How did you meet the beast?" she asked.

"In a field at the back of my house, many, many years ago—when I was about your age, actually," Ebenezer replied. "It got stuck on the bottom of my shoe."

"Blimey—how big was your shoe?!"

"The beast was smaller back then. I thought it was an animal, at first, but then it began to speak. It asked if it could come into the house."

"What did the adults say? Miss Fizzlewick always used to stop me from bringing caterpillars and spiders into the house. It was so annoying."

"The adults, my parents, said no, but I snuck it in anyway. I hid it up in our attic on the top floor, and I brought it some food. Nothing too big at first. I took it up leftovers from my own dinner, when I got the chance. It always loved eating meat."

It had been a while since Ebenezer had thought about his younger years. The beast used to be quite a cute little thing. Cute in an ugly, greedy, and evil sort of way.

"The more it ate, the bigger it got," said Ebenezer, now smiling at his own memories. "And as it got bigger, it became stronger. When the beast was about the size of a football, its powers fully returned. The beast would vomit out little presents for me—just small things, you know, like croquet sets and miniature drums. And in

return, it wanted more interesting meals to eat."

"That's surprising," said Bethany.

"Yes, the beast wasn't always that bad, you know."
Ebenezer nodded. "It's just become greedy, over the years.
And about that, I wanted to say . . . look . . . well, I'm sorry
about what it did with your parents and the smoke, and
everything. I had no idea that it was—"

"That's not what's surprising," said Bethany. "I mean
it's surprising that you brought the beast into the house
even though your parents said no. You seem like such a
Goody Two-shoes."

Ebenezer nearly crashed the car.

"I am not a Goody Two-shoes!" he shouted.

"Yeah you are. I know that you had nothing to do with
the smoke, because you're too well behaved. You might as
well have a pair of shoes that say 'Mr. Goody' on them."

"I am not a Goody Two-shoes. I am a Mr. Naughty
Shoes!"

Bethany looked at Ebenezer. There was a quiver in
her voice as she asked, "Are you saying that you *did* have
something to do with the smoke then?"

"No, no—gosh no. I'm not that sort of Naughty Shoes,"
he said. "Like I said, I am terribly sorry about—"

"I really, really don't want to talk about it!" snapped Bethany.

They didn't speak again until they were pulling up to the house. Ebenezer's curiosity got the better of him.

"Final question, I promise," he said. "Why did you apologize to Geoffrey?"

Bethany chewed her bottom lip.

"It's because I don't want to be like the beast," she said quietly.

Ebenezer parked the car outside the house. Bethany jumped out and ran to the front door. She came back to the car when she noticed that Ebenezer wasn't moving.

"What are you doing?" she asked.

"Driving to the comic-book shop," he said. "You deserve a present for being good."

"Can I get a pet instead?" she asked.

"Absolutely not," he answered. "Now jump in, before I change my mind."

The Comic and the Cushion

Ebenezer and Bethany returned to the house two hours later, each carrying a sack on their back. Bethany's sack contained comics about unruly children, pranksters, and mischievous goblins who enjoyed ruining princesses' parties, while Ebenezer's was filled to the brim with ones about superheroes and cowboys.

They dragged their sacks into the front room and began to read. Neither of them talked, because they had done quite enough of that already. Occasionally one of them would chortle or gasp at what they were reading, and the other one would say, "Shhh!"

As Ebenezer read, he felt his eyes begin to tire. The words and pictures turned blurry, and he had to fetch the

gentleman's monocle that he hadn't worn ever since it had gone out of fashion over a hundred years ago.

"Hahaha! You look ridiculous," said Bethany, when she spotted him squinting through it.

"I thought you were trying to be good," said Ebenezer.

"I am. Aren't good people supposed to be honest? I'm telling the truth—that thing makes you look ridiculous!"

"You might be right," he said, as he caught sight of his reflection. "But I won't be wearing it for long. My eyes will be strong again once I have the potion."

Ebenezer went into the kitchen and made Bethany a large dinner—one that would fatten her up nicely for the beast. He fried a slab of red meat in one pan and boiled a small bucket of potatoes in another.

"Dinnertime!" he shouted, once it was ready.

Bethany stomped to the kitchen table, carrying a goblin comic under her arm. She held the comic open with one hand and forked potatoes into her mouth with the other.

"That looks interesting," said Ebenezer.

The front cover of the comic was a picture of a bright green goblin with orange boots and pointed yellow teeth.

"You can't have it," said Bethany. "It's mine."

"I know it is. I bought it for you. And I don't want it now anyway—I'll just borrow it after you're done with it."

"No."

"No?"

"Yes. No."

"What do you mean *no*?"

"I mean—no."

"But I bought them for you!"

"Yes, and I said thank you—which was very unlike me—and now all the ones in the sack are mine."

"You didn't actually say the words 'thank' and 'you.' And do you mean that you're not going to let me read any of them?"

"That's right. I don't like sharing."

"Well, in that case, you're not allowed to read while you're eating dinner."

Bethany shrugged and closed her comic. She started forking potatoes into her mouth at a rapid pace.

"If I lend you one of my comics, will you get me a pet?" she asked, between forkfuls.

"Bethany, I will never, ever get you a pet. Stop asking me about it."

"But why? Don't you want to know what it's like to have one?"

"I already know exactly what it's like," he answered, looking a little uncomfortable. "A few centuries ago I had a charming Cheshire cat called Lord Tibbles. Unfortunately, things did not end well."

"What happened?" she asked, leaning forward with interest. "Was he a scratchy cat? The scratchy ones are my favorite."

"No, no, no—Lord Tibbles was a perfect gentleman. He was kind and he was fluffy, right up until the day the beast decided to eat him."

Bethany's mouth curled into an expression of appalled horror, but Ebenezer wasn't finished yet. He thought it might be a novel sensation to tell her the whole truth about his relationship with the beast—besides, it wasn't like she was going to be alive long enough to do anything about it.

"So you know when I said that the beast conjures treats for people who are good? Well, that was a rotten lie," he said. "I bring the beast food to eat, and it rewards me with magical potions and other rewards."

Bethany's fork fell from her hand and clattered onto the floor. She didn't seem to notice.

"The beast was jealous of Lord Tibbles," explained Ebenezer. "One day, it said it wasn't going to give me any more potions unless I handed over the cat."

"And what did you say?" asked Bethany, spitting out crumbs of potato as she did so.

"I said, 'Goodbye, Lord Tibbles!' and then I chucked it into the beast's mouth," he answered. "I loved that cat, but I loved me more. I wasn't going to let old age kill me, just to save some animal."

Bethany had lost some of her appetite. Thoughts of the beast eating Lord Tibbles made her push the plate away.

"I think I was wrong," she said.

"About the pet idea?" he asked.

"No, about you. I don't think you are a Goody Two-shoes after all."

"Ha! See, I told you so!"

Ebenezer wasn't feeling in such a "Ha!" sort of mood when he saw the look on Bethany's face. She was looking at him in the way that most people looked when they saw the beast. There was fear in her eyes.

Ebenezer didn't like this. He was used to people being afraid of the beast, but he wasn't used to people being afraid of him.

"You know what, actually I think you're right. I suppose I am a bit of a Goody Two-shoes," he said hopefully.

"No, you're not. A Goody Two-shoes would never have fed Lord Tibbles to the beast. You're a . . . a . . . well, I don't even know what type of shoes you are," she said. "Have you fed many cats to the beast?"

"The beast doesn't like to eat the same thing more than once," explained Ebenezer. "And it doesn't find the taste of cat that interesting."

"What else have you fed it?" she asked.

Ebenezer thought about all the things that he had brought the beast to eat—every antique and every animal, all the exotic creatures and all the ancient artifacts. Bethany was still looking at him in a funny, somewhat uncomfortable way, so he decided not to tell her anything too gruesome.

"Oh, just a few things, here and there," he answered. "Nothing that horrid."

"Is there anything the beast *can't* eat?" she asked.

"It said it was allergic to trumpets a couple of days ago, but that might have been a joke," he answered.

"I am going to feed it one, and find out," said Bethany. "Hopefully it'll explode. If it does, then it will serve it right for what it did to me."

"You will do no such thing—without the beast, I'll die! I don't care how much smoke he vomited at you," said Ebenezer.

Bethany didn't reply, because she was still hurt by the memory of what had happened in the attic.

"Sorry, I didn't mean that. And look, I know you don't want to talk about it, but I just want to say one final time that I really am sorry about what happened," said Ebenezer. "And I know that you must miss your parents terribly—"

"I don't, actually," said Bethany.

"There's no need to try and pretend that you don't. It's okay if you—"

"I don't miss them, because I don't remember them," snapped Bethany. "I was so young when it happened, I don't remember the fire, or anything about my life before the orphanage. That's kind of why I wanted the beast to bring them back—I want to know what they were like."

"Oh right," said Ebenezer. "Right, I see. I completely understand."

Ebenezer couldn't imagine what it would be like to have never known one's own parents—his own childhood had been perfectly splendid. More importantly, he couldn't think of any words he could say to make Bethany feel better.

Bethany removed the crumpled photograph from her pocket—the one on the beach with the mustached, baby-carrying man, and the mustacheless, newspaper-holding lady. Bethany flattened it out and showed it to Ebenezer.

"This is the only picture that's left of us. I'm the scowling baby in my dad's arms."

"He looks a bit like you," said Ebenezer, as he peered at the picture again. "There's the same glint of mischief in his eyes. Your mother looks a bit more sensible—anyone who reads newspapers is likely to be well behaved."

"Look closer," said Bethany.

Ebenezer held his monocle over the picture and peered more closely at the woman in the picture. He spotted that there was a very silly-looking comic peeping out between the pages of the newspaper. Perhaps she wasn't so sensible after all.

"Every night, before bed, I look at the photo and imagine what they were like. Sometimes I make up stories about them—my mother the spy, or my dad the astronaut—or sometimes I imagine them as a pair of adventurers who are still trying to make their way back from a dangerous mission to the North Pole," said Bethany.

She smiled sadly. She would trade all the stories in her head for a chance to meet them—even if they turned out to be the dullest people she ever met.

Ebenezer sat in silence, thinking for a moment or two, and searching his brain for some magical combination of words that might make Bethany feel less horrid about the fact that both parents were strangers to her.

Eventually, he said, "You can keep all your comics—no need to lend me any. And you can read them at the dinner table if you like."

It wasn't perfect, and it probably wasn't going to help Bethany feel any better about the fact that her parents were dead, but she seemed happy enough. She grinned and returned to reading about goblins.

Ebenezer, meanwhile, was feeling a little tired. Now that his body was aging, he was feeling more worn out by the day's activities. He bid good night to Bethany and began the slow climb up the stairs.

"WAIT!" shouted Bethany, before he even made it to the first floor. She ran up to him and sighed. "There are three whoopee cushions under your pillow, as well as a toad. You might want to move them before you lie down."

Bethany then stamped her foot and ran back down the stairs, thoroughly annoyed. It was no fun being well behaved.

The Breakfast

Ebenezer woke up the following morning feeling most unwell. When he opened his eyes, everything was blurry, and he had to put on his monocle just to see the duvet. And then, when he let out his morning yawn, his elbows and arms creaked like they were a set of old doors.

He stood up and discovered that his legs were wobbling. They both still worked, but they had lost much of their strength during the night. It took even longer than it had done the day before to reach the bathroom, and when he arrived, he almost burst into tears.

Ebenezer was upset by his reflection. His face was now entirely wrinkled with age.

Just to make himself feel worse, Ebenezer started to

count the number of wrinkles that had appeared on his forehead overnight. He had reached number eight, when he was interrupted by the sound of the beast's bell.

"This day keeps getting better and better," he moaned to the wrinkly mirror.

Ebenezer trudged upstairs. The sound of the bell grew louder and more demanding as he made his way to the top floor.

The beast continued to ring the bell, even when Ebenezer was in the room. It only stopped after Ebenezer coughed in a pointed fashion.

"What in the name of hot biscuits took you so long?" spat the beast. It was not in a jolly mood.

"Terribly sorry, my legs are a bit slow this morning," answered Ebenezer.

The beast targeted its three black eyes at Ebenezer. It burst into laughter.

"Ho ho ho, oh, Ebenezer, is that really what you look like without the potion?" it said. "Gosh, those 511 years really haven't been kind to you, have they?"

The beast was truly tickled by the sight of Ebenezer's new oldness. It laughed and laughed, until it broke out into a coughing fit.

Ebenezer walked over and gave the beast a firm pat on the back. The beast coughed out some stationery (a ruler, a protractor, and a packet of pencils), and then it was back to normal again.

"You shouldn't have made me laugh so much, Ebenezer!" said the beast crossly. "You know how bad it is for my chest. Really, you could have given me some warning before you came up here looking like that."

"Sorry, but I'm afraid that my appearance was a bit of a shock to me as well. I couldn't give you much warning, because I had no idea that I would wake up looking like this. I can't remember the last time I was without the potion for so long."

"April 1902," said the beast. "It was when you took ages to bring me that Baskerville hound to eat. But I don't remember you looking quite this old and rotten."

"Speaking of the potion, I don't suppose there's any chance you might be able to give me a small advance?" asked Ebenezer.

"Yes, yes, yes—that's why I rang for you. How's the child doing?"

"She's doing fine, actually. A lot better. You know, she's not as awful as I thought—she apologized to someone yesterday, and she didn't let me sleep on a toad, so . . . yes. Progress, I would say."

The beast was not impressed. It didn't care about Bethany's emotional journey to becoming a better-behaved person. It only wanted to know whether the child was now large enough to eat.

"The child seemed a little rounder, when I saw her," said the beast. "There was more skin on her bones, and more juiciness in her cheeks. You have done good work, Ebenezer."

Ebenezer blushed. It was always a nice surprise to receive compliments from the beast.

"And you know, I haven't had so much as a bite to eat, since that singing parrot," continued the beast. "My stomach has started to growl."

"Oh, poor you," said Ebenezer. "You should have said. Would you perhaps like a little snack?"

"I would rather a fat child, Ebenezer! How much clearer can I be?"

Ebenezer's chest tightened. He started to feel uneasy.

"Be a dear, and fetch the child," said the beast. "Bring up some of that fancy chutney as well—I want the dish to be oozing with flavor."

"No!" blurted Ebenezer.

"Run out of chutney, have you? How irritating. Well, I guess a few bottles of brown sauce will do."

"No! I won't do it! Not with chutney, and not with brown sauce!" Ebenezer blinked, shocked at his own reply. He'd never said no to the beast before.

The beast gave Ebenezer a stern stare. Its three black eyes shone with fury.

"Please don't tell me you've become attached to that brat. I have already laughed quite enough for one day," said the beast.

Ebenezer thought about what he was doing, and he wondered what had come over him. Why was he trying to help Bethany? He pulled himself together.

"I hadn't finished speaking," said Ebenezer. "When I said that I won't do it, I meant that I won't do it *now*, as in today. You see, it doesn't matter how much brown sauce or expensive chutney you put on Bethany, because I don't think she's quite ready for you to eat. Give me another day to fatten her up."

The fury evaporated from the beast's eyes.

"Thank goodness, you almost had me worried," said the beast. "I thought it was going to be like that pet thing all over again. What was that cat called? Lady Trouble, or something like that? Anyway, I'm very glad that you're doing the right thing."

"Don't worry, there was never any chance that I was going to do the wrong thing," said Ebenezer.

"Good, good. Can I really not eat her today, though? I can feel another growl coming on."

"Trust me, it'll be worth the wait," said Ebenezer. "In the meantime, what did we decide about that potion advance . . . ?"

"We decided that you would get your potion after I've eaten the child, and not a moment before!" said the beast.

Ebenezer hid his disappointment and walked to the door. Before he left the room, he said, "By the way, that cat's name was not Lady Trouble. He was called Lord Tibbles."

There was a lump in Ebenezer's throat as he walked downstairs. For the first time in a couple of centuries he found himself thinking about Lord Tibbles, and he was rather upset as he remembered everything that had happened.

This sudden concern for others was most unusual. Ebenezer could recognize that his own behavior was odd, particularly when it came to Bethany. He had been quite fond of Lord Tibbles, so it was understandable that he would feel upset from time to time, but with Bethany it didn't make sense, because he didn't think he liked her.

Ebenezer should have just given Bethany to the beast. It would have saved him having to tell those lies about her not being ready to eat, and he would have gotten his hands on the potion so much faster. Now, however, he had to spend another whole day with her, and he had to struggle around the place with an aging body.

Ebenezer wondered why he had acted in such a strange manner. He was never normally squeamish about feeding things to the beast, so why hadn't he brought Bethany upstairs?

Ebenezer blamed his body. Older people tend to be more emotional about things, and this concern for others was probably a side effect of the wrinkles and the weak legs. He was sure that all these unusual feelings would disappear once he had the potion.

When Ebenezer walked into the kitchen, he was greeted by the sound of Bethany snoring. She was lying in a face-down starfish position, under a blanket of crumpled comics.

Ebenezer laid out the bowls of porridge, the jugs of orange juice, and the baskets upon baskets of croissants and mini muffins. He banged a spoon on a saucepan to wake Bethany up.

He took a seat at the breakfast table and discovered that Bethany had left something for him at his place. It was the comic with the cover of the orange-booted, yellow-toothed, bright green goblin, and she had put a Post-it note on it, which read:

Fine, you can borrow it.
But if you don't give it back,
I'll ruin all your favorite sweaters.

Ebenezer was touched. He couldn't remember the last time anyone had let him borrow something.

"Thank you," he said to Bethany, as she sleepily took her seat at the table.

"I mean it about the sweaters," she said. "If you don't give it back within a week, then I'm going to feed them to the moths."

122

Bethany picked up a plate and filled it with two pains aux raisins and half a dozen mini muffins. Ebenezer noticed that she had already gained quite a lot of weight. If the beast saw her, it would eat her on the spot.

"Maybe you don't need to eat quite so much food today," said Ebenezer. "You might live longer if you eat more healthily."

"Bog off," said Bethany. Then she shoved two muffins into her mouth.

The Bucket List

Ebenezer did not bog off. He refused to move from his seat, and he defied Bethany by scooping some porridge into his bowl.

Meanwhile, Bethany made herself a squashed-muffin sandwich—a new dish that she had recently invented. She laid a blueberry muffin on top of a pain aux raisins, bashed it into little pieces with her fists, and then put another pain aux raisins on top. She picked the whole thing up, careful not to let any crumbs get away, and then she scoffed it all down in three greedy bites.

It was quite a sight to see, and Ebenezer didn't know whether he should be impressed or appalled. As he looked at her, he realized that this was going to be the last day of her life. Tomorrow, she would be nothing but a digested meal at the bottom of the beast's belly.

"What are you looking at?" asked Bethany.

"Sorry for staring," answered Ebenezer.

"I can make you one if you like," she said, grabbing another two pains aux raisins. "Which flavor do you prefer? Blueberry or chocolate?"

"Oh no, I'm fine, thanks."

Bethany's face fell. She was disappointed.

"Go on then, I'll try one," said Ebenezer. "Blueberry, please."

Bethany's face jumped back into place. She unwrapped a muffin, beat it to death, then scattered the corpse between two pains aux raisins. There was a tinge of nervousness, as she presented the finished product to Ebenezer.

As soon as Ebenezer bit into it, he knew it was going to be nasty. There's a reason why muffins are not usually used as sandwich fillings.

"What do you think?" asked Bethany hopefully.

"It's *delicious*," he lied. "Really wonderful."

"Great!" Bethany beamed with joy. "I'll make you another one!"

"Oh no, no, no—please, no. I'm already stuffed."

Bethany shrugged and returned to her own squashed-muffin sandwich. She dipped it in one of the bowls of porridge to improve the flavor, and then immediately regretted the decision.

As Ebenezer looked at Bethany, and thought again about her impending death, he came to the conclusion that she was not an entirely horrible person. After all, there must be a smidgen of good in someone who is capable of sharing both their comics and their unusual sandwich recipes.

If this is to be the last day of Bethany's life, thought Ebenezer, *then I am going to make sure that it's a good one.*

"Do you have a bucket list?" he asked her.

"I don't have any lists. And if I did, I wouldn't write them on a flipping bucket."

"No, that's not what I meant."

126

"It's what you said. You should think about your words more carefully next time."

Ebenezer went on to explain that a bucket list is a list that has nothing to do with buckets, and everything to do with death. He explained that everyone has things they want to do before they die, and that these things, when thought about or written down, make up a person's personal bucket list.

"That's stupid," said Bethany. "It should be called a death list instead."

"It's called what it's called, because the first person who made one was a big fan of buckets. His one goal in life was to build the world's largest bucket—one that would be able to hold an entire mountain of rocks."

"And did he?"

"Nope, and he didn't even come close. The one he made was barely large enough to hold a pebble. But, you see, that's the thing with bucket lists; people rarely get to do everything that they want to do in life."

Bethany wondered why Ebenezer was suddenly so interested in talking about death. She noticed that he looked a lot older than he had the night before.

"Are you about to die or something?" she asked. There

was a hint of irritation in her voice, as if she thought Ebenezer was being selfish for choosing to die.

"Gosh no," said Ebenezer. Then he thought about it. "Well, actually, I suppose yes, I am. Right now, I'm currently on my way to dying of old age. But that'll all be fixed when the beast gives me the potion."

"And when will that be?"

"Tomorrow, I think. But anyway, enough about that. I want to know if there's anything on *your* bucket list."

Bethany frowned with concentration.

"I suppose there may be one or two things . . . ," she said.

+   +   +

There were more than one or two things on Bethany's list, and Ebenezer tried to make sure that they got through as much of it as possible. A few of the things she wanted to do, such as riding to the moon in a helicopter made of jam, were not practical; however, there were plenty of things that they were able to tick off.

The day began with a trip to Buckingham Palace. Bethany had heard that the Queen's horse guards (those red chaps with the big silly hats) never laughed in public, and she wanted to see whether this was true.

She made Ebenezer stop to buy a joke book on the way, and then, when they arrived outside the towering gates, she started to read from it. The horse guard on duty didn't crack so much as a smile, even when he was faced with some of the more hilarious ones, like . . .

What do you call a magic dog?
A labracadabrador.

and

What do you call an elephant that doesn't matter?
An irrelephant.

and even . . .

Why did the golfer wear two pairs of pants?
In case he got a hole in one.

The complete absence of giggles disappointed Bethany. She felt that she couldn't remove Buckingham Palace from her bucket list until she had made a horse guard laugh. Ebenezer saw this and decided to help.

He started tickling the horse guard with his handkerchief.

Still, there was nothing. The horse guard was well trained and didn't make a sound, even when Ebenezer became more aggressively playful with his handkerchief.

The tickling business was brought to an end by the arrival of Perkins, the Queen's chief under-butler. He informed Bethany and Ebenezer that the Queen was most unhappy with their behavior, and that they were no longer welcome to talk to her horse guard.

"Idiot!" Bethany shouted at Ebenezer, as they walked away. "Now I'll never be able to make one laugh!"

Bethany was so angry, in fact, that she bashed Ebenezer's bottom with the joke book. Ebenezer was unprepared for this and promptly fell flat on his face.

"Ho ho ho!"

Bethany and Ebenezer looked behind them in surprise. Both of them could have sworn that the sound had come from the horse guard, but he gave no sign of having let out a laugh—his face was back to being stern and horse-guard-like.

"Do you think that counts?" asked Ebenezer.

"Oh yeah, that definitely came from him," said Bethany.

Ebenezer and Bethany high-fived. They were about to leave, but decided to stay because they noticed that the Royal Marching Band was putting on a performance.

The band marched from the doors of the palace, through the towering gates, and out into the public arena. They were playing a triumphant song to mark the half-birthday of the Queen's favorite corgi.

Everything was going terribly well, and all the band members were looking very pleased with themselves. But then the performance came to an end after Bethany appeared to attack a member of the brass section.

Perkins returned and removed Bethany from the band member. He handed Ebenezer a note from the Queen, which read:

Her Majesty formally requests that you cease lingering outside her residence. Henceforth, she would be most obliged if you would refrain from visiting all royal locations.

"You what?" asked Bethany.

"It means we need to bog off, Bethany," explained Ebenezer.

He and Bethany returned to the car and quickly zoomed away from the palace. Ebenezer took the opportunity to ask Bethany to explain what in the name of fudge cake she had been thinking.

"I was trying to get his trumpet," said Bethany.

"His trumpet?"

"Yeah—so I can shove it down the beast's throat. No one vomits smoke at me and gets away with it."

"Please don't," said Ebenezer. "I'll remind you once more that I'm only able to stay alive because of the beast."

Bethany made no promises to follow Ebenezer's instructions. During their ride back, they were able to tick off another two items from Bethany's bucket list: they pretended to be Russian while ordering from a drive-through restaurant, and they composed a song using nothing but the car horn.

Ebenezer had prepared himself to have a thoroughly miserable day. He'd imagined that the task of going through Bethany's bucket list would be a boring one filled with childish and uninteresting activities. And so he was surprised when he realized that he was having a wonderful time. He decided that if he ever had to feed another child to the beast, then he would definitely let the child have a bucket-list day.

"So what next?" asked Ebenezer, excited for the next activity.

"I think you know," said Bethany, with a grin.

Ebenezer paused to think about what delightfully wicked activity might be up Bethany's sleeve.

"Are we going to make some prank calls?" he suggested.

"No, but that's an awesome idea—let's add it to the list. What I want to do next . . . is get a pet!"

"Bethany, there's no point getting a pet. You'll only be able to look after it for a day."

"Why only a day?" Bethany was puzzled. "What's happening tomorrow?"

Ebenezer thought quickly, wondering how he would be able to backtrack. It would really spoil the day if she found out that she was going to be eaten alive tomorrow.

"I mean, you won't be able to keep a pet in the house without the beast eating it," said Ebenezer. "Remember Lord Tibbles."

"I won't let it eat my pet!" declared Bethany.

"The beast will order me to bring it the pet, and I won't have a choice in the matter."

"That's total rubbish," said Bethany. "You don't have to do everything the beast says."

"I'm afraid I do. If not, I will die of old age. The beast has complete control over me."

"Maybe it's better for you to die than live getting bossed around by that thing," she snapped. Then, after about five seconds, she added, "Sorry, I didn't mean that."

The mood had soured. All the jolliness of the day was slowly disappearing out of the car.

"Don't worry about it," said Ebenezer. "I know it's hard to understand, but the beast and I . . . well, we need each other. Now, aside from the whole pet thing, is there anything else left on your list that we can do?"

"I really, really want a pet. Or at least to have a look at some animals. Can't we go to a zoo or something?"

"Unfortunately not, because I recently received a lifetime ban from the head zookeeper," said Ebenezer. "But I do have another idea. . . ."

The Birdless Cage

E benezer led Bethany into the bird shop. They were soon greeted by the large and pleasant bird-keeper.

"Hello, hello, welcome to the finest and most special-est bird shop in the world!" said the bird-keeper. It was a sentence that he used to greet all new customers.

"Don't you recognize us? I've been here several times, and you sold Bethany some worms," said Ebenezer.

The bird-keeper peered into Ebenezer's face, as if he were inspecting the plumage of a rare bird. Eventually, it dawned on him.

"Oh, it's Mr. Tweezer!" he said. "Sorry for not recognising you sooner, but you don't look like you usually do. Have you had a haircut?"

"No, I've just lost control of my body. Don't worry, I'll soon have a potion for it."

"Ri-ight," said the bird-keeper, not quite sure how to respond. He turned his attention to Bethany. "You owe me ten worms, miss. That backpack you gave me was useless."

"So were those worms. They kept wriggling out of Geoffrey's nostrils," said Bethany. "I'd like five new ones, please."

"And I'd like a brand-new backpack!"

"I'll settle for two and a half."

"You'll settle for nothing!"

The bird-keeper wondered why Ebenezer had picked such an argumentative child. He was sure that the orphanage would have had some far nicer ones to choose from.

"Sorry to interrupt," said Ebenezer, as Bethany was about to lower her offer to one and three quarters of a worm, "but we're on a bit of a tight schedule. Do you mind if we cut straight to business?"

"Of course," said the bird-keeper. "But if you've come about the society finches, then I'm afraid to say that I ain't got any left. Mr. and Mrs. Cussock got the last ones this morning."

"No, no, no—it's not about that. In fact, it's not about a specific bird at all. We're not looking to buy anything," said Ebenezer.

The bird-keeper's face fell. His favorite thing about Ebenezer's visits was always the money he got at the end of them.

"My friend Bethany here wants to see some animals, and we're looking for something a bit more personal than the zoo. We were wondering whether you would perhaps be able to give us a little bird tour?" asked Ebenezer.

It was a most unusual request. The bird-keeper had never been asked to do such a thing before.

"I'd love to help, Mr. Tweezer, I really would, but I have a business to run. If you're not looking to buy anything today, then I'm afraid I ain't gonna be able to help you. Bird tours are not something that I—"

Ebenezer silenced the bird-keeper by laying a pile of notes on the counter.

"But as you're such a good customer, I'd be happy to help, Mr. Tweezer!" said the bird-keeper, beaming. "Come on through!"

"Did you just call me your friend?" Bethany asked Ebenezer as they were led through to the back of the shop.

"Yes. I suppose I did," he answered. "It's funny, I don't remember the last time I referred to anyone as a friend."

"What a loser," she laughed. Then, a few moments later, she added, "Don't think I've ever had a real friend either. You can be my first, if you like."

Ebenezer stopped as a most unusual warm feeling filled him from top to toe.

"Hurry UP, loser!" Bethany called over her shoulder.

The first bird on the tour was the hoatzin, a rare, extremely smelly bird with claws on its wings and a spiky hairdo of feathers at the top of its head.

"Would you like to feed it?" asked the bird-keeper.

Bethany nodded determinedly.

"Go and fetch those flowers by the till for me then."

"I don't think flowers are going to make it smell any better. Wouldn't it be more useful if we fetched some perfume?" suggested Ebenezer.

Bethany returned with the flowers—a delightful bouquet of lilacs, daffodils, and sweet peas. The bird-keeper opened the hoatzin's cage and motioned for Bethany to put them in.

The hoatzin's eyes widened and its nostrils flared with excitement. It took one or two sniffs of the flowers, then

opened its beak and started wolfing them down. Ebenezer
gasped, while Bethany giggled.

"The hoatzin is a South American herbivore," explained
the bird-keeper. He saw Bethany was confused, so he added,
"Herbivore basically means that it doesn't eat meat. Loves

flowers and plants, and all that. Part of the reason why it smells, actually."

"Does plant eating make it smelly?" asked Bethany.

"Sort of. It has a stomach like a cow's and it digests its food very slowly, and in a way that lets out a lot of nasty smells. I've had it for years, 'cause I ain't been able to find anyone who wants to bring the smell into their house. Anyway, I ain't got all day—time for the next one."

The next one was a long-beaked, red-eyed creature with black feathers and razor-sharp talons. The sign on its cage read: THE FANTASTICALLY FEROCIOUS EAGLE.

"The name's a joke," explained the bird-keeper. "As a matter of fact, it's probably the gentlest bird in the whole building. Unlike most eagles, it ain't a predator, and it doesn't really need much food. One grape is enough to see it through for an entire week. Speaking of which . . ."

The bird-keeper removed a green grape from his jacket pocket and gave it to Bethany. He removed the Fantastically Ferocious Eagle from its cage and gently placed it so that it was perched on Bethany's shoulder.

"Are you sure that's a good idea?" asked Ebenezer, as he looked at the razor-sharp talons.

"Trust me, Bethany couldn't be safer," answered the bird-keeper.

"Yeah, mind your own beeswax," added Bethany.

She stroked the black feathers of the Fantastically Ferocious Eagle and fed it the grape. A small, happy smile formed around the Fantastically Ferocious Eagle's beak, and it rubbed its belly with its wings. It looked like someone who had just eaten a five-course feast.

"Will that really last it a whole week?" asked Bethany.

"Oh yes. If it ate any more, then it wouldn't feel too good. Its species evolved to live on hardly anything," said the bird-keeper.

Bethany rang her fingers along the bird's talons, and then she returned to stroking its feathers. After a few strokes, the bird shut its eyes and let out a gentle snore.

"The Fantastically Ferocious Eagle must feel comfortable with you," said the bird-keeper. He gently removed the Fantastically Ferocious Eagle from Bethany's shoulder and returned it to the cage. "It doesn't sleep on just anyone."

Next on the tour were the parakeets; a pair of small, round, colorful birdies who got on so well that the bird-keeper said that he would only ever sell them as a pair.

Then came the agoraphobic homing pigeons, and after that were the hummingbirds and the tutting ducks. The bird-keeper let Bethany hold and feed all of them.

Ebenezer had never seen a child look so happy. He was amazed that Bethany could take such joy from something that didn't involve pulling a prank or saying something rude. He decided that she deserved to take one of them home.

"I've been thinking," he said to her, as she fed a king-fisher a worm. "Maybe if we keep it very, very quiet, and we make sure that the beast doesn't find out, then we might get away with it."

Bethany's eyes lit up. "Do you mean . . . ?" she asked.

"Yes. If you like, we can take one home with us," he answered.

Now it was time for the bird-keeper's eyes to light up. "Which one do you want?" he asked. "They're all *very* reasonably priced."

Bethany looked at all the birds that had gone before. She had enjoyed seeing the parakeets tweet excitedly at each other, and the tutting ducks had made her laugh a lot, however, there was only ever going to be one winner. She pointed at the Fantastically Ferocious Eagle.

"An excellent choice," said the bird-keeper. "You'll

save a fortune on bird feed as well, Mr. Tweezer. I'll go and get it for you now."

"Wait a minute," said Bethany. "What about the rest of the tour?"

The bird-keeper sighed; he was impatient to get his hands on the money. He rushed through showing Bethany and Ebenezer the rest of the birds. He didn't let Bethany hold the doves, because he said that they were pretty but far too boring to interest her, and he didn't give them any interesting facts about the toucan.

When they got to the final cage, the bird-keeper said, "Well, this one doesn't need any introduction."

The final cage was empty. It was labeled with a sign that just read PATRICK.

"Is it an invisible bird?" asked Bethany, as she peered into the cage.

"Mr. Tweezer! You don't mean to tell me that you ain't introduced her to Patrick yet?" asked the bird-keeper.

Ebenezer looked sheepish. Then he looked at the floor.

"Who's Patrick?" asked Bethany.

"Why, only one of the most rarest, most wonderful-est birds!" exclaimed the bird-keeper. "It's a Wintlorian purple-breasted parrot—less than twenty of them left in the world. He can sing any song; human, birdy, and everything else. Have you gotten him to sing you any Elvis yet, Mr. Tweezer?"

"No, no, I haven't," said Ebenezer, still refusing to move his eyes from the floor.

"You should. He does a lovely 'Burning Love.'"

Bethany walked over to Ebenezer and tapped him on the arm. He ignored her, knowing what was coming. He hoped just to leave here swiftly with the Fantastically Ferocious Eagle before having to answer any tricky questions. But Bethany kept tapping until Ebenezer eventually looked up from the ground. His eyes were filled with regret.

"What happened to Patrick?" asked Bethany.

"Um . . . I'm afraid . . . well, he's no longer . . . exactly . . . alive," he said.

"What?!" exclaimed the bird-keeper. His bottom lip wobbled with sadness. "How is that possible?! He was the best and truest bird that I ever knew!"

All the birds in the room who understood English were most offended when they heard this.

"I just don't understand!" continued the bird-keeper. "He was so kind and so healthy. How could this have happened?"

"I think I know," said Bethany quietly. "And I think it wasn't pleasant. Your birds are wonderful, but I don't think I want to take any back into Ebenezer's house."

The Needy Orphans

It's amazing how quickly a day can change. Less than five minutes beforehand, they had all been feeling pretty jolly about life.

"I ain't feeling jolly about life," moaned the bird-keeper.

"Neither am I," said Bethany.

"I'm also far from jolly," added Ebenezer.

Like most un-jolly people, all three of them wanted to have some time alone with their thoughts. The last thing any of them wanted to do was make conversation, and so it was highly irritating when they heard the shop door swing open.

"Good day!" shouted a voice, which was infuriatingly chirpy. When you are feeling un-jolly, there is nothing worse than having to deal with someone who is in a good mood.

Ebenezer, Bethany, and the bird-keeper stumbled to the front of the shop. They discovered that the owner of the chirpy voice was Miss Fizzlewick, and that she had arrived with a box. Each of them groaned. She was unable to tell that her presence was unwelcome.

"Good day to all of you!" said Miss Fizzlewick. "Well, two of you anyway," she added, on spotting Bethany. "Have you had a haircut, Mr. Tweezer?"

"No, I'm just an old fart," he answered grumpily.

"Why are you here?" asked the bird-keeper, even more grumpily.

"That's a very good question!" shrieked Miss Fizzlewick. Her enthusiasm was relentless. "And the answer is that I want to offer you the chance to feel good about yourself."

The bird-keeper perked up at this.

"As you probably already know, at the Institute for Gentlemanly Boys and Ladylike Ladies, we can't always give as much as we would like," said Miss Fizzlewick. "What with all the money it takes to feed the children and clothe them and keep them in school, we don't have much left to treat them."

"Ever," muttered Bethany.

Miss Fizzlewick narrowed her eyes but carried on. "Yes, well, we can't always give them the presents and rewards for good behavior that *some of them* deserve."

"Your office seemed awfully nice for someone who can't afford presents," said Ebenezer.

"I am a lady, Mr. Tweezer, and I have grown accustomed to ladylike things. My luxurious lifestyle is a necessary expense for the orphanage," said Miss Fizzlewick.

The bird-keeper was losing interest. He couldn't see how any of this would help him feel better about the fact that his favorite bird had died in suspicious circumstances.

"Now then, you're probably wondering what this all has to do with you," continued Miss Fizzlewick, addressing the pressing issue. "Well, I have been visiting all the business owners in the area, and I have asked them all whether they have anything they might be able to donate to us."

Miss Fizzlewick put her box on the counter and showed some of the things that had already been donated. The items in the box included twelve bags of licorice from Miss Muddle's sweetshop, a stack of unwanted books from the local library, a bottle of full-fat milk from the milkman, and a trio of trumpets from Mr. and Mrs. Cussock's theater school.

"And so now, I come to you," said Miss Fizzlewick to the bird-keeper. "Is there anything you might be willing to give to those who need it most?"

"But Miss Fizzlewick, this is a bird shop!" protested the bird-keeper.

"That hardly matters," said Miss Fizzlewick. "Surely, in all your shop, there must be at least one thing you can share?"

This sort of request would never have usually worked with the bird-keeper. He was a money-minded businessman, and he was not in the habit of giving away his birds for free. However, on this day, he was suddenly struck with a wonderful idea.

The bird-keeper went to the back of the shop and returned, a few moments later, with the hoatzin. He placed it in Miss Fizzlewick's box and smiled.

"It's all yours," he said.

Miss Fizzlewick's nose wrinkled as she was struck by the bird's stench. "Do you have anything a little more . . . gentlemanly or ladylike?" she asked.

"Nope. Just this one," answered the bird-keeper. "Don't you want it?"

"Oh yes, of course we want it," said Miss Fizzlewick. "It would be terribly ill-mannered to say no. It's just that, um, well, actually this box is pretty heavy, so maybe it's best if I come back for this, er, lovely . . . really, really lovely bird later."

"That's all right, I'll leave it out for you. What time will you be back?" asked the bird-keeper.

"Ooh, well, actually, you know, I have quite a busy schedule what with the orphans and . . . and the other orphans. You should put that lovely, really, truly lovely bird . . . back where it came from, and I'll come and collect it after I've given all these other things to the children."

"Great," grumbled the bird-keeper. "I can't even *give* this bird away."

Ebenezer and Bethany bid a glum farewell to the bird-keeper and left the shop. They reached the car and were surprised to find that Miss Fizzlewick had followed them.

"Can we help you?" asked Ebenezer.

"I thought you'd never ask!" said Miss Fizzlewick, jumping into the front seat. "Just so you know, I can only stay for one. The children will expect me back soon."

Ebenezer took the driving seat, while Bethany climbed into the back, still too glum to even kick the back of Miss Fizzlewick's seat.

"Stay for one what?" asked Ebenezer.

"Cup of tea!" barked Miss Fizzlewick. "A lady never drinks anything stronger before nighttime."

"Right," said Ebenezer. "So you're coming back with us, are you?"

"Why yes, of course! You need to help me fill my box, and then you're taking me back to the orphanage."

Deciding that he didn't have a choice in the matter, he drove them back home. Miss Fizzlewick ensured that there was no quiet time during the journey, as she talked continuously at Ebenezer. She did this, in spite of the fact that Ebenezer didn't even pretend to be interested in what she was saying.

"By the way, Geoffrey's been asking after you," she said to Bethany, as they all got out of the car. "Although I can't think why he would want anything to do with you, after all you've done to him."

Bethany didn't respond. Once they were inside the house, she announced that she was going to the living room (alone) to read some comics.

"You know, Bethany, it's actually more polite to *ask* whether you can read the comics. You should show some respect to Mr. Tweezer," said Miss Fizzlewick.

"Bog off, Miss Fizzlewick," said Bethany.

"I beg your pardon!" said Miss Fizzlewick. She looked to Ebenezer, expecting him to do something about it.

"Bethany, show some manners to our guests," sighed Ebenezer.

"Fine then," said Bethany. She walked over to Miss Fizzlewick and looked her straight in the eyes. "Bog off, Miss Fizzlewick, *please*."

Bethany left for the living room, and Ebenezer headed for the kitchen. Miss Fizzlewick was left speechless and gasping like a goldfish.

"Which tea?" shouted Ebenezer. "Earl Grey, Darjeeling, peppermint, Banoffee pie, green, white, purple, or honeyed lemon?"

"Yes," said Miss Fizzlewick.

Ebenezer shrugged. He filled a mug with tea bags from all the various boxes. Meanwhile, Miss Fizzlewick took a look around the place.

"This is quite a house. I'm sure there'll be plenty here for my box and me," she said, gazing eagerly up the stairs. "Shall we begin the tour?"

"It's fifteen stories high, and my legs are tired," said Ebenezer.

"We better start straightaway then!" said Miss Fizzlewick. She started climbing up the stairs, without waiting for any further response from Ebenezer.

During the tour, Miss Fizzlewick would walk into a room, criticize everything she saw, take an occasional item or two for her box, and then move on to the next one. Ebenezer was remarkably patient; however, his nerves were tested when they reached the eleventh floor.

"This is clearly all wrong," said Miss Fizzlewick. "What were you thinking when you purchased these pictures? That woman's nose is on backward, and that skeleton is smoking a cigarette! It's not very family-friendly, now, is it?"

Miss Fizzlewick walked over to the picture of the golden boy, and it was here that things got truly tense.

"What nonsense!" she said. "I've seen orphans draw more interesting pictures with their fingers. This house is in serious need of a lady's touch."

"This house does not need to be touched by anything!" said Ebenezer. "And *The Golden Boy* is one of the finest pictures that has ever been produced by mankind. Your children would chop off their fingers for a chance to paint like that!"

"You must calm down at once, Mr. Tweezer," she said, giving him a stern *Aren't you a naughty boy?* sort of look. "A gentleman never loses his temper."

They continued the tour up the next three flights of stairs. Miss Fizzlewick began to grow impatient with the lack of box-worthy items on offer.

"Is that the last one?" she asked, pointing to the stairs that led to the beast's room. "My box isn't even half full. It's all gone by far too quickly!"

Ebenezer had just been thinking the exact opposite and wondering whether time was passing deliberately slowly, just to annoy him. He stood in front of the staircase to stop Miss Fizzlewick from going any further.

"Actually, we're stopping here," he said. "There's nothing up there that will interest you."

Miss Fizzlewick ignored him. She pushed past Ebenezer and marched up the stairs.

"I think I'll be the judge of that, thank you very much," she said. "It's probably where you store all the good stuff."

"No, wait—stop!" Ebenezer shouted.

He tried to catch her, but his legs weren't moving fast enough. She swung open the creaky old door and pointed into the room.

"What do we have here?" she asked.

The Noisy Curtains

That is none of your business," said Ebenezer.

"It looks like a pair of red velvet curtains," said Miss Fizzlewick.

She walked over and inspected them more closely. She felt the soft, plush fabric between her fingers and gave them a sniff.

"Why, Mr. Tweezer, these will go perfectly in my office!" she said. She quickly corrected her mistake. "I mean, in the orphanage, of course. It's a well-known fact that all children love curtains."

"Excellent idea," he said. "I'll buy you a set of curtains like these for every room in the house. Let's go down there, immediately, so I can give you the money."

But Miss Fizzlewick wasn't done with her search. She bent down to the curtains again and placed her ear to them.

"Is there something behind here?" she asked. "I could have sworn that I just heard a noise. It's a sort of grunting, snuffling sound."

"The sound is neither a grunt nor a snuffle!" said the beast, in its loud and slithery voice. "It is the sound of a majestic and beautiful being that will expand your definition of life itself!"

Miss Fizzlewick looked to Ebenezer. She wasn't used to having her definition of life expanded. In response, he rolled his eyes.

"Stand back as far as you can, Miss Fizzlewick," he said. "Don't shout, don't scream, and don't make any unpleasant noises. This is going to be a bit of a shock."

"Mr. Tweezer, there's nothing behind those curtains that I haven't seen a thousand times before," she said.

Ebenezer pulled open the curtains. Miss Fizzlewick tried her best not to be shocked, but she still let out a gasp and dropped her mug, which crashed onto the floor and smashed into pieces. She quickly regained her composure and tried to act like it was no big deal.

"Ah yes," she said, looking at the beast. "I think I saw one of these before, when I was in Paris."

"You did not," slithered the beast.

"Perhaps it was when I was holidaying in Budapest," she said.

"I don't think you saw anything like this in Budapest, Paris, or anywhere else in the world except this room, Miss Fizzlewick," said Ebenezer.

"Why? Is it a rare creature?" asked Miss Fizzlewick.

"I am the last of my kind," boasted the beast.

As head of the orphanage, Miss Fizzlewick was used to dealing with children who had lost their families. She said exactly the same thing to the beast as she said to everyone who came through the orphanage's doors.

"You mustn't whine and grumble. Everyone loses some-one at some point, and it's very annoying and selfish if you try to make a big deal of it," she said. Then, to soften the blow, she asked, "What happened to the rest of your kind?"

The beast looked to its belly and smiled. Miss Fizzlewick didn't understand what it was trying to say, so she replied, "It's good that you're taking it so well. You're very sensible."

"What else am I? Aside from sensible," asked the beast.

Miss Fizzlewick looked to Ebenezer. He offered no assistance.

"Well, you're gray. You have black eyes. And you're quite large," she said.

"I am not large! I am thin, beautiful, and I have recently been exercising!" said the beast. "And that's not what I meant. Tell me what I'm *like*."

"I'm sorry, but I just don't know. We've only just met."

This was not what the beast wanted to hear, but Miss Fizzlewick didn't care. "Where do you keep your cleaning equipment?" she asked Ebenezer. "A lady never leaves a mess lying around."

"Third floor. Fifth door on the right from the staircase—next to the stationery suite," he replied.

"There's no need to go all the way down there," said the beast. It closed its eyes, shut its mouth, and hummed and wiggled. Then it vomited out a dustpan and a brush.

"Crikey!" said Miss Fizzlewick, using a word she hadn't spoken in almost twenty years. "How did you do that?!"

"Very easily," replied the beast. "So. What do you think I'm like now?"

"You're certainly an interesting one. And I must say,

that was most impressive," enthused Miss Fizzlewick. "Play your cards right, and I might put you in my box."

"Well done," purred the beast. "That was a much better answer."

"I'd like to bring the children to see this—it would be such an interesting experience for them," she said.

"I don't think that's a very good idea!" said Ebenezer hurriedly.

"I think it's a wonderful one," said the beast, licking its lips using both tongues.

"So do I. Don't worry, I'm sure we can persuade Mr. Tweezer soon enough," said Miss Fizzlewick.

She bent down and started brushing shards of mug into the dustpan. After about three sweeps, her work was interrupted by a grunty growl that came from the beast's stomach.

"I'm rather hungry," explained the beast, with a wicked little smile. "Ebenezer's been awfully cruel and has left me without a bite to eat for quite some time."

"Mr. Tweezer! That is most ungentlemanly!" said Miss Fizzlewick.

"We mustn't be too harsh on him, though," said the beast. "He has spent the last few days preparing me an

162

absolutely delicious meal, so he's not all that bad."

"Well, that's more like it," she said. "What food do you enjoy eating?"

"All sorts. I'm not a fussy eater, and I always like to try new things," said the beast.

"That's an excellent attitude. I wish more of the children had your appetite. They can be quite ungrateful, you know."

Miss Fizzlewick finished clearing the floor. The beast's stomach made two more groany growls.

"Take this to the nearest bin, Mr. Tweezer," she said, handing Ebenezer the dustpan.

"Er, yes. Why don't you accompany me downstairs— right away—and I'll show you where it's located!" answered Ebenezer.

"Oh, there's no need to leave just yet," said the beast. "Just put it back in my belly—I don't mind."

"Won't the broken bits of mug hurt you?" asked Miss Fizzlewick.

"My belly is very strong. Come and have a look."

Miss Fizzlewick walked over, and the beast opened its mouth wide. She dropped the dustpan and brush into his mouth, and then she put her head inside to have a proper look.

163

"Why are there so many purple feathers at the bottom?" she asked.

The beast's open mouth curved into a smile. It wrapped its two tongues around Miss Fizzlewick and dragged her into its belly.

"No! Spit her out right now!" shouted Ebenezer.

It was no use. The beast crunched down on Miss Fizzlewick until eventually the only sound left in the room was the happy purr of the beast.

In all his 511 years of existence, Ebenezer had never seen anything so horrid.

"What a lovely snack," said the beast. "It was very thoughtful of you to bring one up for me, Ebenezer."

The Inconvenience

"Stop looking at me like that," said the beast. "You're acting like you've never seen me eat a meal before."

Ebenezer was as pale as a glass of watery milk. His fingers were twitching, and his knees were trembling.

"N . . . n . . . never seen you eat a human," he stuttered, between a series of deep and jangly breaths.

"Humans, cats, statues of Winston Churchill—they're all the same. I don't know why you're getting so worked up about it," said the beast. "Although, I must say, this one tasted wonderful. Mmmnnnh! It was everything I was hoping for."

The beast smiled and looked down at its full belly. It burped out Miss Fizzlewick's ears, which bounced along the floor and landed by Ebenezer's feet.

"Be a dear and pop those back into my mouth," said

the beast. "They were one of my favorite parts of the meal. After the nails and the kneecaps, of course."

Ebenezer didn't pop the ears back into the beast. In fact, he didn't move at all—he just stayed quivering and staring at the beast in a horrified manner. His heart was beating so fast, his whole chest was shaking.

"Oh, all right, fine then," said the beast. "I suppose you're right. I shouldn't spoil my appetite before tomorrow's feast."

"So . . . you still want to eat Bethany?" asked Ebenezer. "You're not too full to appreciate her?" he asked hopefully.

"Why yes, of course I'm going to eat her, you fool. That Fozzlewocklewhatever woman was just the appetizer!" said the beast. "And I must say, I'm itching to get my mouth around the main course. It'll be interesting to see what younger, fresher meat tastes like."

"I need to go downstairs," said Ebenezer.

"Good plan, you need a lie-down—you're not yourself at all, old boy."

Ebenezer picked up Miss Fizzlewick's box and went downstairs, but he didn't lie down. He went straight to his thinking chambers, a series of extravagantly decorated rooms, which were located on the eighth floor. He sat on one of his many thinking chairs and took a moment to come to terms with the terrible thing he had just seen.

Ebenezer had seen the beast eat all manner of live animals—from baby kangaroos to old, grizzled polar bears to Lord Tibbles the cat—and he had watched it bite and tear its way through several ancient objects. It had never been pleasant to watch the beast at mealtimes, but nothing had ever been anything quite like what he had just seen.

He hadn't fed Miss Fizzlewick to the beast, but he hadn't done enough to stop it from happening, either. And now, with all that he had been doing to prepare Bethany for the beast, he realized that he was about to let something similar happen again.

There was a burning, gnawing at the pit of his stomach, and it took a few minutes for him to realize that he was feeling guilty again.

It can be rather a nasty shock when you realize that you've been behaving badly. The feeling is not unlike the one you experience when you look in the mirror and find out that the leopard-print onesie you've been wearing all day doesn't actually suit you.

The gnawing, burning in Ebenezer's stomach grew more and more painful, as he started remembering all the things that he had brought the beast to eat over the years. All the whines, squeaks, and tweets sounded in his ears, and every surprised face he had seen flashed before his eyes.

Ebenezer had always seen the beast as the evil one, and himself as the helper who had no choice over what he was doing. Now, however, he realized that this was not the case. Every time he had decided to help the beast, in order to get a potion or a present for himself, he had committed a dreadful deed. At any time over the past five hundred years, he could have chosen to stop helping the beast, but instead, he had been selfish and cruel.

The feeling of guilt was so overpowering that Ebenezer felt he could no longer stay sitting down. He needed to do something to interrupt his train of thought, so he picked up Miss Fizzlewick's box and continued his descent down the stairs.

After a brief pause on the third floor, where he stopped to make a visit to his designated crying room, Ebenezer headed to the ground floor. He went into the downstairs sitting room to distract himself with some television, before realizing (too late) that Bethany had already taken over the comfiest sofa.

Much to his surprise, she wasn't reading comics. Her legs were crossed and her face looked cross. There were crayons and pieces of paper scattered around her.

"How could you have done that?" she asked, with a frown on her face.

Ebenezer gulped. He wondered how she had found out about Miss Fizzlewick so quickly.

"I can't believe you fed that talking, singing parrot to the beast," she continued. "That was a rotten thing to do."

Ebenezer breathed a sigh of relief. He dropped the box on the floor and took a seat on the sofa next to Bethany.

"Yes, it was," he said. "And I'm sorry. I know that I've done some pretty nasty things in my life, and I wish I could take them back."

Bethany was surprised. She had expected an argument and was unprepared to deal with an apology.

"Right. Well. Good," she said. "I've written you a letter to tell you how terrible you are."

She picked up one of the pieces of yellow paper and handed it to Ebenezer. He started to read it.

Dear Geoffrey,
I hear you've been thinking about me, and I want you to know that I've been thinking that maybe you're not such a terrible rat after all. If you're free and would like to read some comics together one afternoon—

"Not that one!" said Bethany, when she realized her mistake. She snatched the paper and tried to hide the fact that she was blushing.

She searched the sofa for the right piece of paper, and then double-, triple-, and quadruple-checked she had the right one before handing it over. Ebenezer peered closely at the paper.

"Sorry, but I can't make out a word of this," he said.

"Neither can I," said Bethany, when she tried to read it. "Sorry, my handwriting isn't very good when I'm angry. Suppose I'll just have to tell you what I want to say."

Bethany cleared her throat. She got up and stood underneath the huge television on the wall, as if she were about to deliver a show.

"It is not nice to feed animals to the beast, especially if they are talking, singing parrots. In fact, it is not nice to do anything nice for the beast, because it is a horrible, evil, mean, nasty, not nice thing," she began. "You are a bad person because you help the

171

beast. But you are also the most good bad person I know.

"It was kind of you to give me those comics, and to let me eat whatever I want whenever I want it. Today's bucket-list day has also probably been one of the best days of my life—so, you know, well done on that. I don't believe in hugs, but I will allow you to pat me on the head, if you would like."

Bethany took a step forward and bent her head. Ebenezer obligingly gave it a pat.

"Most importantly," she concluded, "I can forgive you for all those things you've done for the beast, because you haven't given it anything to eat since I've been in the house. I'm trying to be better behaved, and I think you should try it too. Together, maybe, we could help each other be good. What do you think?"

Ebenezer paused. He knew that being a good person means that you tell the truth.

"The beast is hungry, and you're next on the menu. I only adopted you so that I could feed the beast a child," he said. "I really am terribly sorry about the inconvenience."

The Stupid Idiot

Ebenezer told Bethany everything. He explained that he had adopted her because she seemed like a horrible girl who deserved to be eaten, and he told her that he had fed her mountains of food because the beast wanted something fat to eat.

It was tricky for him to confess the truth, but it was even trickier for Bethany to hear it.

"But why?" was the only thing she could say, after he had finished speaking.

"Because the only thing I've ever wanted from life is more life," he said, bitterly. "More things, more years to live, more good looks—more everything! You're a child, so you have no idea how scary it is to get older.

"This is my worst nightmare," he said, pointing to his own old body. "I've always been terrified of aging, of losing my looks, of dying before I've had a chance to do everything I want to do. So when the beast offered me a chance to keep on living, in return for a few small favors, I immediately said yes."

"Small favors?" said Bethany, in a small voice. "There's nothing small about feeding it a child."

"It didn't start out like this. At first, all the beast wanted me to do was bring it some interesting meals to eat—some plates of roast beef and a chicken pie or two—that sort of thing. Then it wanted to know what it was like to eat living things, first insects, then small animals like rats and pigeons. And as it got bigger, so did its appetite.

"There were times when I was uncomfortable, like with Lord Tibbles, but my life was always more important to me than anything else."

"And what about me? Am I another Lord Tibbles?" asked Bethany.

"No. You're *much* worse than Lord Tibbles," he answered. "Lord Tibbles was a kind and noble cat, whereas you . . . you think it's funny to ruin paintings, steal comics, and demand obscene amounts of chocolate cake. If you were an ounce like Tibbles, then I would never have picked you at the orphanage."

Bethany was a tough girl, but she wasn't tough enough to hold back the tears that trickled from her eyes. It's never nice to hear that someone thinks you deserve to be eaten.

"But . . . but I thought you liked me?" she asked, in a wobbling voice.

"I didn't. In fact, I was looking forward to serving you to the beast," said Ebenezer. More tears trickled from Bethany's eyes, and a sob escaped from her throat. Ebenezer stood up and sighed. "But, for some ridiculous reason which I really don't understand, I like you now."

Bethany looked up. There was a glimmer of hope in her tear-sodden eyes.

"Very unfortunately, you're not quite as awful as I wanted you to be," explained Ebenezer. "And, I suppose, you're actually quite fun to spend time with. I think that maybe, just maybe, as silly as it sounds, this house and my life might feel a little empty if you weren't in it."

Ebenezer and Bethany looked at each other and smiled. Then Bethany punched him in the stomach.

"You stupid idiot!" she shouted, punching again. She

kept punching until he fell back on to the sofa. She picked up a cushion and started bashing him over the head with it. "How dare you try and feed me to the beast! How dare you say those nasty things about me!" she said, bashing him over the head again and again.

It was time for tears to trickle from Ebenezer's eyes. He had never been very good at dealing with pain.

Bethany kept bashing and shouting and bashing and shouting until her arms and voice could bash and shout

no more. She slumped into the seat next to Ebenezer, out of breath and out of insults. They both stayed sitting there for a while; Ebenezer shed tears of pain, while Bethany let out ones of anger.

"What do we do now?" she asked, after the tears had dried.

"Run away," he answered. "There's nothing else to do."

"Where are we running to?"

"Not sure. Haven't given the plan much thought."

Bethany smiled. Running away from somewhere was one of the last items left on her bucket list.

"Do we really have to leave the house?" she asked. "It's not like the beast can chase after us."

"The beast can move when it wants to, and there's no telling what other tricks it has got stored in its belly. No, it's far too dangerous for you to stay. Go upstairs, fetch a suitcase, and be careful not to give the beast any sign of what's happening."

Bethany went up to the fourth floor and paid a visit to the luggage room. After a few minutes of searching, she finally selected a black rucksack and a small brown suitcase with the initials P. B. on them.

"What do the letters stand for?" she asked, when she returned downstairs.

"Peruvian Bear, or something like that. Belonged to a charming little chap who I brought to the beast about a year ago," said Ebenezer. He paused. "Gosh, I really am a terrible person."

While Bethany was upstairs, Ebenezer had made a pile of things in the downstairs sitting room that he thought she might find useful. The pile contained a change of clothes, a few slices of chocolate cake, a pair of binoculars, and a fly swatter.

Ebenezer went to his safe, which was located behind one of the fridges, and opened it. It was lined with neat stacks of thousand-pound notes. He filled Bethany's rucksack, until the zippers were almost at bursting point.

"That's about a million pounds. Should hopefully be enough to last you for a couple of weeks," he said.

"How are you so rich?" asked Bethany. "Are you a bank robber?"

"No. It's all from the beast. Now, shh, we don't have time for questions," he said.

Ebenezer packed Bethany's suitcase with the pile of things, and added a few other items, including a few of her unread comics and a package of cookies. He picked up Miss Fizzlewick's box and brought it over to the suitcase.

"Is there anything in here that you want?" he asked.

"Thought we didn't have time for questions," she answered.

"Shh, we don't have time to make clever jokes. Or stupid ones, for that matter!"

Bethany looked inside the box, which contained the twelve bags of licorice, the unwanted books, the milk (which was now beginning to smell), the three trumpets, and the various items that Miss Fizzlewick had tried to steal for her office. There was nothing inside that would be worth carrying around.

"Won't Miss Fizzlewick want these?" asked Bethany. "Where is she anyway?"

"Dead, I'm afraid," said Ebenezer. "Sorry, I should have told you sooner. The beast ate her and I couldn't do anything to stop it. Are you upset?"

Bethany wasn't. She had never liked Miss Fizzlewick or her obsession with ladylike behavior, so she really wasn't sad, but she thought she probably should be.

"Oh yeah, of course," lied Bethany. "Very sad."

Ebenezer hadn't liked Miss Fizzlewick that much either,

but he felt a need to play along. "Gosh, it really is a pity she's gone," he said. "She was such a *wonderful* person."

They were both quiet for a moment or two, as they wondered how much time they should leave before changing the topic of conversation. Bethany was the first to break the silence.

"I really didn't like the sound of being eaten," she said.

"Yes, the sounds of someone being eaten are usually horrid. Lots of screams and yelps. Glad to help you escape it."

"Have you decided where we're going yet?" she asked.

"*We* are going nowhere. You'll have to go alone," he said. "There's no telling what the beast will do once it finds out what's happened. I'll stay here to distract it. Besides, my body is too old to do any sort of running—I'd only slow you down."

"But what's gonna happen to you when I go?"

"I'll probably make myself a cup of purple tea and head to bed. And then, I suppose, at some point tomorrow, I'll join Miss Fizzlewick in the land of the dead."

Bethany gasped. She knew that Ebenezer was getting older, but she hadn't had any idea that he had so little time left.

"Oh there's no need to worry," he said. "512 years is

more than enough for me. Come on then, off you pop."

Ebenezer opened the door for Bethany and motioned for her to leave. He was putting on his best brave face—determined not to reveal how scared he was of death—but it didn't work. Bethany saw right through him.

"I'm not going," she said.

"You are," he said firmly. "I'm ordering you to leave."

Bethany shrugged off her backpack and emptied the contents of her suitcase out onto the floor. She slammed the door that Ebenezer was trying to hold open.

"I've never been very good at following instructions," she said. "And I'm not going to let you die alone."

The End of Ebenezer

Ebenezer woke up the next morning feeling pretty sorry for himself. He had begged Bethany to leave, but she wasn't having any of it. Every time he attempted reasoning with her, she just folded her arms and blew raspberries at him.

Ebenezer was also feeling sorry for himself because he was looking and feeling like someone who should have died a few centuries ago. His limbs were aching, his eyes were barely working (even with the monocle pushed right in his eye), and there wasn't a part of his body that wasn't infested with wrinkles.

He would have happily spent the day in bed, groaning and feeling sad, but Bethany had other ideas. She burst into the room with a saucepan and started whacking it with a wooden spoon.

"Wake up, wake up, wake up!" she shouted.

"I'm already awake. Leave me alone," he groaned.

Bethany did no such thing. She started jumping on the bed and continued to whack away at the pan. With great effort, and little enthusiasm, Ebenezer sat up.

"What is it?" he asked.

"I wanna save your life. I stayed awake all last night, and I have some ideas," said Bethany. She fished in her pocket and brought out a crumpled piece of paper.

"Dear Geoffrey . . . ," she began, before realizing that she had the wrong one. She fished out another sheet from her back pocket. "Idea number one—let's take you to the hospital."

"Doctors can't help me, only magical potions can. People aren't meant to live to 511, you know," answered Ebenezer. "Also, I don't like hospitals or medical equipment."

"Fine. Idea number two—why don't we offer the beast something to eat instead of me?"

"Already tried that," said Ebenezer. "And it's only interested in you, I'm afraid."

"Humph. Well, it doesn't matter because my third and final idea is an awesome one anyway. Why don't we try and force the beast into giving you your potion?"

Ebenezer sighed. He looked at Bethany and wondered how she planned on overpowering a magical, all-consuming creature.

"Here's what I'm thinking," she said. "We go to the orphanage and borrow some of the children. There are ones like me there—proper naughty ones who aren't afraid of a fight. Then, if you buy us all some catapults and rotten apples, we storm upstairs and attack the beast until it gives you what you need. What do you think?"

"Utter rubbish. Doesn't work on any level," said Ebenezer. "The beast can't be forced to do anything.

"Okay, I've just thought of a totally wicked fourth idea," she began.

"Great to know, but I'm not quite sure that I want to spend my last day on earth hearing about ideas that will never work. Let's go downstairs."

This was easier said than done. It took about twenty minutes for Ebenezer to stand up from the bed, and another good half an hour or so to crawl into the bathroom. By the time he got there, he didn't have the energy to brush his teeth, so Bethany grabbed the toothpaste from the sink and squirted some into his mouth.

Ebenezer continued to crawl, and with Bethany's help, they made it downstairs. He was exhausted by the time they reached the kitchen.

"Whatcha wanna eat?" asked Bethany.

This was a surprisingly difficult question to answer. It's a strange thing to choose what you want to eat for your last-ever breakfast on the planet, and Ebenezer was filled with questions. Did he want porridge? Would a croissant prove a better choice? Should he go all out and treat himself to a spot of fried kipper?

Ebenezer dithered for too long, so Bethany made the decision for him. She brought out a plate of squashed-muffin sandwiches and a cup of purple tea. This was not the meal that Ebenezer had in mind, but before he could make a complaint, their breakfast was interrupted by an unpleasant noise.

The beast was ringing its bell.

Ebenezer's and Bethany's faces grew a little paler. Both did their best to ignore the sound, but it felt wrong. Ebenezer had spent the best part of five hundred years answering its every call, while Bethany found it impossible to try and ignore a creature that planned to eat her alive.

The bell continued to ring.

Ebenezer's heart pounded in his chest and beads of sweat oozed from his wrinkled brow. Bethany bit her lip to stop herself from screaming in terror. They both longed, more than anything, for the ringing to stop.

And then, after about ten minutes, it did. The silence was even worse. It made them suspect that the beast was up to something horrid.

"What do you think it's doing?" asked Bethany.

"Planning its next move," answered Ebenezer.

They listened for the return of the bell. But the sound never came.

"That's probably good news, isn't it?" asked Bethany. She didn't believe her own words.

"Yes, I suppose it must be," said Ebenezer, even though he knew it meant nothing of the kind.

He bit into his squashed-muffin sandwich. He was too focused on the beast to worry about how his last breakfast tasted.

"Maybe this means that the beast is trapped up there?" asked Bethany.

"Maybe," answered Ebenezer. "Or it might mean—"

Their breakfast was interrupted again, but this time by a sound that was far closer and more disturbing to their ears. The baby grand piano, the one that the beast had vomited out for Ebenezer to put in his front window, was playing a song. The tune was loud and lacked melody—it was the sort of noise a piano makes when a cat is dropped onto its keys.

Bethany and Ebenezer looked at each other, confused, and then they got up to inspect the piano. As they came closer to it, the music grew louder and angrier. The keys on the instrument seemed to have a life of their own.

"How's this happening?" asked Bethany.

"It's the beast," said Ebenezer. "It must have some control over the things it creates."

Then, as if to agree with Ebenezer's point, the piano started to walk. It scraped its legs, leaving deep marks and scratches on the floor, and moved toward Bethany and Ebenezer. The piano's movements were slow and uncoordinated, but they were still terrifying.

Ebenezer and Bethany quickly backed away, back into the kitchen, but an unpleasant surprise was waiting for them there as well. Mugs and teapots started leaping out of cupboards, flying at their heads, and smashing into the floor and the walls.

Meanwhile, the fridges were out of control. Their doors swung open and shut and they started hurling their contents at Ebenezer and Bethany. The dessert fridges were particularly aggressive and successfully managed to knock Bethany over more than once with a well-aimed soufflé.

"We have to get out of here!" she yelled, making a somewhat obvious point.

Unfortunately, the piano seemed to know what Bethany had in mind, and scraped its way to the front door so that it could block their escape route. The dessert fridges detached themselves from the walls and blocked the other exits in the house.

"Quick, help me into the sitting room," said Ebenezer. His voice was faint with exhaustion.

Bethany and Ebenezer hobbled into the downstairs sitting room. They were chased every step of the way by a flying selection of mugs, cutlery, and other household appliances. Once they reached the front room, Ebenezer slammed the door shut, and Bethany dragged a table and an armchair over to make sure it couldn't be opened again.

"Why's it gonna be any better for us in here?" asked Bethany.

Ebenezer was too tired to remain standing. He slumped onto the sofa and let out a long, pitiful groan. His eyes began to droop.

"Ebenezer, this is not the time for napping!" shouted Bethany.

"Trust me, we're safer in this room," said Ebenezer, in a voice that was fainter and croakier than ever. "Hardly anything in here came from the beast's belly. I bought most things with money from the beast instead. You'll need to get rid of *some* stuff, though."

The "some stuff" included a set of snow globes, a footstool, a dressing gown that was hanging off the back of the door, a flowerpot that had no flowers in it, and a game of Ludo. Bethany shoved and locked them into a trunk that was sitting at the back of the room, just as the objects were starting to come to life.

"Good, I think that's everything," said Ebenezer.

He should have thought harder. The television switched itself on. It was too high on the wall for Bethany to reach, and Ebenezer's heart was beating far too fast for him to even think about standing up.

For a few brief moments, Ebenezer and Bethany thought that the television might not be an issue. All it did at first was play a cartoon featuring a crime-solving hat and a villainous scarf.

"Ooh, I like this one!" said Bethany.

But then the images on the screen turned gray and started to blur. The dramatic fight scene between the hat and the scarf was replaced with an image of the beast's black eyes, which were shining with fury.

"Oh, I don't like this one," said Bethany.

The beast took a step back so now nearly its whole face was in view. It leaned forward and stared from the screen.

"EBENEZER! WHERE ARE YOU, EBENEZER? I'M SOOOO HUUUUNGGGRRRREEEEE!" it shouted.

Ebenezer didn't answer, and the beast didn't seem to be able to see what was happening on the other side of the television.

"IF YOU'VE DIED ON ME, EBENEZER, I'M GOING TO KILL YOU!" shouted the beast, with a hoarse voice. It stopped shouting, and all Ebenezer and Bethany could hear for a while was its angry, impatient breathing.

Bethany picked up the remote control and tried changing the channel back to the cartoon. Then, when this didn't work, she tried switching the television off, but it kept switching itself on again.

"Unplug it!" said Ebenezer.

This didn't work either. The images of the beast in its attic stayed on the screen. The beast began to speak again, this time changing its approach.

"Bethany . . . Oh, Bethaneee!" it cooed. "Come up,

little Bethany! Has Ebenezer been a silly sausage and died? Come up to see meeee and I can bring him back to life."

Ebenezer shook his head. He couldn't believe that the beast was stooping so low.

"Ooh, and Bethany, guess what? I've figured out how to bring your parents back to life. Come up and see meeeee, and I can whisper the secret into your ear. Come hear, little Bethany!"

Ebenezer shook his head more vehemently.

"Hellooo, Bethany," said the beast in a strange, high-pitched voice. "I'm your mummeee. The beast has brought me back to life, come up and see meee! Gosh, the beast is such a clever, wonderful, charismatic, charming, extraordinary . . ."

Ebenezer shook his head with such force that he worried it might fall off. Bethany, meanwhile, dug through Miss Fizzlewick's box until she found the glass bottle of (now absolutely stinking) milk. She carefully aimed it and threw it at the television screen.

The glass bottle smashed into pieces, but also smashed the screen. The stinking, milky liquid mingled with the electricity, and the television started to fizzle and spark in a most unhealthy way. Still, though, the images of the beast continued to roll.

"Oh, Bethany!" boomed the beast, now doing its best impression of a father's voice. "Come to Papa!"

"You'll never see her!" Ebenezer shouted back, even though he knew there was no way that the beast would be able to hear him. "She's gone far away from here!"

"Okay, little Bethany—I'm going to come down to yooooou."

Ebenezer gulped. Bethany let out a pained squeal. The beast waddled out of view, only to waddle back a few moments later. Syrupy sweat rolled off its fat body, and it looked frustrated.

"WELL. I CAN'T BE EXPECTED TO WALK DOWN FIFTEEN FLIGHTS OF STAIRS," it bellowed. "COME UP HERE IMMEDIATELY, BETHANY!"

Bethany didn't go up there immediately. Instead, she said, "Whoopee!" and enjoyed a wrinkly high five with Ebenezer.

The beast was fuming. It stomped its feet, and its syrupy sweat boiled with anger until it turned to steam. Ebenezer and Bethany couldn't stop themselves from laughing at its helplessness.

The laughing stopped when the beast let out a wicked little smile and started to wiggle and hum.

First it vomited out a bag of bricks, which it placed

to its right. Then came a bowling ball the size of a small moon, which it placed to its left. Finally, it produced a two-hundred-pound weight, which it placed immediately in front of its body. The beast was now surrounded by three incredibly heavy objects, and the floorboards started to creak.

"What's it doing?" asked Bethany.

The beast started to jump. On its third jump, the floorboards gave way, and the beast and the objects disappeared, as they fell through to the fourteenth floor.

"Oh no, please no," said Ebenezer.

The beast continued to vomit out heavy objects and jumped its way through one weak floor to another. Soon, it was just two floors from reaching Bethany and Ebenezer.

"We're doomed!" said Ebenezer. He clutched his chest, as his heart gave out entirely and he collapsed onto the sofa. Bethany ran over and tried to wake him up. She shook his body and slapped his face, until the last moments of life flickered in his face. "I'm so terribly sorry," he murmured. "It's all my fault. I should never have brought you into this house."

Ebenezer squeezed Bethany's hand, and then all signs of life disappeared from his body. His breathing stopped, his eyes collapsed shut, and his wrinkly skin faded to an unpleasant gray color.

"OH, BETHANEEE!" shouted the beast from the hallway, after it burst through the final ceiling. "THE BEAST WANTS TO SAY HELLOOO!"

Tears poured from Bethany's eyes, and snot streamed from her nose, but she knew what she needed to end this. She let go of Ebenezer's lifeless hand and walked over to Miss Fizzlewick's box. She grabbed one of the trumpets and shoved it down the back of her trousers.

She was ready to face the beast.

The Beast and the Bethany

The beast smashed the door open with the moon-sized bowling ball and used the two-hundred-pound weight and bag of bricks to push the other obstacles to one side. It made the piano play another loud, nasty tune as it waddled into the room.

"Mmnh!" it said, as it sniffed the air greedily. "There's a delicious smell of death about the place!" It followed its nostrils and noticed that the scent was coming from the fresh corpse of Ebenezer. "Poor Ebenezer. It's such a pity—he's one of the better servants I've had over the past thousands of years."

"It's not a pity, it's murder!" said Bethany. "If you had given him the potion, he would still be alive."

The beast turned its attention to Bethany. It licked its lips when it saw how big she had grown. "My, my, my, Ebenezer fed you well," it said in its soft, slithery voice. "You're as fat and juicy as a ginormous strawberry."

"You still look like a big blob of gone-off mayonnaise," answered Bethany.

"Ignorant brat! Can mayonnaise do this?" asked the beast. It wiggled, and hummed, and vomited out a gnome.

"No, and I wouldn't want it to. It would totally ruin my chips," answered Bethany. "Also, if I wanted one of those, I could just order one from the garden center."

"Foolish child! Can your precious garden center deliver this?"

It wiggled and hummed and vomited out a thumb-sized triangular bottle, containing a peculiar-looking blue liquid. The sight made Bethany raise her eyebrows.

"That is the elixir of life—a magical potion containing all the vitamins needed for youth, life, beauty, and shiny hair. It's so powerful, even I can't control it, like I do with the piano and all the other things," said the beast, mightily pleased with itself. It paused to think for a moment. "I wonder whether it could bring Ebenezer back. It's going to be such a pain finding someone else to bring me my meals."

"It's a bit—" Bethany began.

"Impressive? Mind-boggling? Applause-worthy?" The beast looked most smug.

"No. I was going to say that it's a bit—"

"Better than a garden center? More extraordinary than a spoonful of mayonnaise?"

"No! Frankly, it's a bit . . . small," Bethany said.

The mood hadn't exactly been toasty, but now it dropped by another few dozen degrees. The beast was not one of those creatures who was responsive to feedback.

"Small?" asked the beast. "Sorry, did you say the magical, age-defying, life-redefining potion was *small*?"

"I actually said a *bit* small," said Bethany.

"I'll have you know that I gave that potion to Ebenezer and it kept him young and beautiful and shiny-haired for an entire year!" roared the beast. "And I can make as much of it as I like!"

The beast proved its point by wiggling and humming and vomiting again. The end result was another triangular, blue-liquid-filled bottle, which was the size of an entire hand.

"That one contains enough liquid to keep someone young and beautiful and shiny-haired for an entire decade!" boasted the beast.

Bethany shrugged. She pretended not to be impressed. The beast vomited again, this time producing a triangular bottle the size of an entire arm—one large enough to hold seventy years' worth of potion doses.

"That's more like it," said Bethany.

She could see the potion more clearly, now that it was in a bigger bottle. It swirled around with an electric energy and seemed to have a mind of its own. The beast sat down, because it was rather tired out by all the waddling and vomiting.

"Come and take a closer look, if you like," said the beast.

Bethany took a step forward and the beast's three black eyes sparkled with excitement. She stopped, and then took a step back.

"I know what you're trying to do," she said.

The excitement in the beast's eyes was now replaced with irritation.

"I'm trying to give you a better look at these magical potions," it said.

"No, you're trying to get me to come closer so you can eat me," she replied.

The beast laughed a slithery fake laugh, which lasted far longer than it should have, and included about seventeen *hehehes*, a dozen *hahahas*, and two long *hohohos*. At the end of its performance, it asked, "Eat you? What would give you an idea like that?"

"Ebenezer told me everything."

The irritation was replaced with indignation. If its eyes had been able to spit, then they would have done so in fury.

"That rotten, treacherous twit. I'm glad he's dead! It's like the cat all over again, the stupid fool," said the beast.

"It's not like the cat at all. We were friends," said Bethany. "In fact, Ebenezer told me I was the first real friend he ever had."

"What?!" The beast felt betrayed by Ebenezer. "I gave him presents and he brought me food. Isn't that what friendship's about?"

"Friendship's about so much more than that, you stupid blob. It's about bucket lists and squashed-muffin sandwiches. It's about not putting toads under your friend's pillow, and it's about—"

"You seem to have confused me for someone who cares," said the beast. It waved its tiny hands and the dessert fridges came into the room to stop Bethany from running away. They opened and shut their doors in a menacing manner, while the piano began another horrible song. "I'm going to eat you, and there's nothing you can do to stop me."

"I don't wanna stop you," said Bethany. "I wanna make a deal."

The beast laughed again, but this time the *hehehes*, *hahahas*, and *hohohos* were real. It was amused by Bethany's comment, and it decided to let her live a little longer so that it could enjoy hearing her suggestion.

"I'm gonna let you eat me. And in return, I want you to try and bring Ebenezer back to life," said Bethany.

"You're going to *let* me eat you?" laughed the beast. "I have you surrounded—there's no way you can escape me or *stop* me eating you. Anyway, there's no guarantee that potion will work. I've never tried using it to bring somebody back to life before."

"If you don't try and save Ebenezer, I'll make it tricky for you to eat me. I'll run, I'll duck, and I'll jump. You and your dessert fridges will have to waddle as fast as you can to keep up with me—it will be exhausting, and it will be messy. Surely you'd rather eat your first child in one delicious bite?"

The beast grimaced, as it realized that Bethany was right. Without Ebenezer around to restrain her, it was going to require a lot of effort to get her into his belly. It also thought that the taste of self-sacrifice might add an intriguing flavor to the dish.

"A deal's a deal," said Bethany. "Ebenezer brought me into the house, and now you're going to eat me. It's only fair that you try and help him live."

Bethany stepped forward so that she was now two steps away from the beast's mouth. Its nostrils flared with excitement, and thick gray dollops of dribble oozed out of the corners of its mouth.

"Do you have any idea what you're offering?" it asked.

"Yes—it's all pretty clear to me," said Bethany.

"I don't think it is. I don't think you have the faintest idea what is about to happen."

"Well, I know you're going to eat me, and I think that just about covers it."

"Oh, it's so much worse than that. Let me explain," it said. "First, I will drag you into my belly with my tongues, and then I will start gnashing.

"There's no telling what I might eat first. It might be your bottom, or one of your toes. There's only one thing that's certain—you will die in great pain, and in the end, the only thing left will be a pile of mushy bones. Now do you still think that you want to step inside my mouth?"

"I don't," she said, taking another step forward. "I'm doing this because I want to save Ebenezer."

The beast was happy to hear this.

"Fine, it's a deal," said the beast. "I will eat you, and then, if by some miracle the potion brings Ebenezer to life, I will let him live. He's more useful to me alive anyway."

Bethany had gotten her way, and she was now within a single step of becoming the beast's next feast. She hesitated.

"Hurry up," said the beast. "The longer you leave it, the less likely the potion will work."

Bethany knew what she had to do to save Ebenezer. She put her hands behind her back and took the step forward.

"Bon appétit," said the beast.

It spread its dribbling mouth wide open. Bethany pulled the trumpet out from the back of her trousers and threw it down the beast's throat. She was about to find out exactly what it meant to be allergic to trumpets.

The effect was immediate. The beast tried to spit it out, but it was already too late.

Its mouth snapped shut. There was fear and fury in its three black eyes, and steam poured out of its nostrils.

A great churning sound came from its belly, and its skin stretched to the breaking point.

Then it shrank smaller and smaller—like a deflating balloon—and it wiggled uncomfortably from side to side. After ten seconds, it was the size of a bag of rubbish, and after ten seconds more it was no bigger than a football. The piano stopped playing its song, and the fridges switched off.

It was a fascinating sight, but Bethany didn't have time to enjoy it. She picked up the nearest bottle of potion (the small one), and raced over to Ebenezer. She opened his mouth and poured every drop down his throat.

For a few moments, nothing happened, and Bethany worried she had done something wrong, or that she had arrived too late. But then Ebenezer came to life with a cough.

And as he coughed, the wrinkles started disappearing from his face, and the color returned to his hair. After a few more coughs, he was strong enough to stand up. He blinked at Bethany, utterly confused.

"But . . . what happened?" he asked.

"Trumpets and elixirs," answered Bethany, which made him even more confused.

"What about the beast?" he asked.

"Good point," she answered.

Bethany turned around to look down at the beast, but there was no sign of it. "Did you kill it?" asked Ebenezer.

"No idea," answered Bethany.

They walked over to where the beast had been sitting and looked closely on the ground. The beast was there and just about still alive, but it had now shrunk to the size of a worm.

Ebenezer bent down and picked it up by one of its legs. It still had three eyes and two tongues, but everything was minuscule. It was shouting angrily in a voice that wasn't loud enough for either of them to hear.

"What do we do with it now?" asked Bethany.

The Final Meal

The bird-keeper was wearing his most serious outfit. It was a black suit, with a white shirt and a loosely tied gray tie. He stood behind the till, next to a handwritten sign that read BIRD TOURS FOR SALE—MOST REASONABLE PRICES.

"I thought you said you didn't do tours?" asked Bethany.

"You and Mr. Tweezer inspired me. Customers have been flooding through them doors since I started doing them. Still ain't got rid of the bloomin' hoatzin, though," he answered, while an exotic bird sang a beautiful song in the background.

The song was a cheery, toe-tapping number, which the bird had been singing for a few hours. Bethany and the bird-keeper were happy to pass the time listening to it, while they waited for Ebenezer to park the car.

He came in a few moments later. He looked young and beautiful, and his hair was immensely shiny.

"You've had another haircut, haven't you, Mr. Tweezer?" asked the bird-keeper. "This one looks much better."

"Thank you."

Ebenezer noticed the sign. "I thought you didn't do tours?" he asked.

"Well, I do now," answered the bird-keeper. "And business is booming."

"Why didn't you dress up like that when you gave us our tour?" asked Bethany.

"This isn't for the tour," said the bird-keeper. "It's to mark a very sad occasion. We're holding Patrick's funeral today."

Ebenezer realized that the beautiful song in the shop reminded him of Patrick.

"It sounds a bit like him," said Ebenezer. "Did he record an album before . . . well, before what happened?"

"No. That's Claudette singing. She's a cousin of Patrick's," said the bird-keeper. "She came to visit this morning, and I had to tell her the bad news. So in true Wintlorian tradition, she began the funeral singing immediately."

Ebenezer poked his head around the back of the shop and saw that Claudette didn't just sound a bit like Patrick—she

looked a bit like him too. Her chest was purple and her talons were green; however, she was shorter and just a teensy bit rounder than her cousin.

"The song's a bit too happy for a funeral, don't you think?" said Bethany.

"Maybe a little. But she's a wonderful singer," said Ebenezer.

The three of them stood listening to the song for a few moments. The music transported each of them to a different place inside their head.

The bird-keeper was the first to break the lull in the conversation, because he had listened to the song for a while and because he was a businessman who didn't like to leave customers standing aimlessly in his shop.

"Was there anything in particular you wanted?" he asked.

"Yes, actually, we're looking for—" began Ebenezer.

"It's Ebenezer's birthday today," interrupted Bethany. "Do you do any birthday discounts?"

The bird-keeper flinched at the use of the word "discount." Then he was struck by a wonderful idea.

"We do even better than discounts. We give our most special, most loyal customers presents on their birthday!" he said.

The bird-keeper turned to go to the back of the shop, but Ebenezer stopped him.

"Sorry, but I don't want the hoatzin for my birthday," he said. "Thanks for the offer, but we're not actually here to buy a bird."

The bird-keeper turned back to face Bethany and Ebenezer. He was unhappy.

"Mr. Tweezer, you know this is a bird shop, and yet it's the third time this week you've come in and you ain't wanted a bird," he said. "First you wanted a kid, then you wanted a tour, and now what? An igloo? The meaning of life? A hippo-bleedin'-potamus?"

"If it's not too much trouble, we would like a cage. The most powerful one you've got, please," said Ebenezer.

"Well, I guess that's all right," grumbled the bird-keeper. "So it's for a strong creature, is it?"

"One of the strongest," said Ebenezer. "As strong and as dangerous as a baby elephant in the midst of a temper tantrum."

"Right. You'll be needing the Pamlex cage for that then. I use it to house the kicking cassowaries, if I ever have one in."

217

"Sounds perfect," said Ebenezer.

"It won't come cheap, mind," said the bird-keeper, with glee in his eyes.

"Money is not an issue," said Ebenezer.

"Those are my four most favorite words," said the bird-keeper. He went to the back and returned a few moments later, carrying a large cage with iron bars and an oversized padlock. "What do you think?"

"Terribly sorry to be a pain, but that's not quite what we're looking for," answered Ebenezer. "Do you have any smaller ones? Perhaps one without the spaces between the bars as well?"

The bird-keeper humphed. It hadn't been easy to drag the Pamlex cage all the way from the back. "You got any pictures of the creature? It would be good to know what kind of size we're talking about," he said.

"We've got the creature with us!" said Bethany excitedly. She fished in her pockets and produced the beast, who was still no larger than the size of a finger.

The bird-keeper was not amused. He was no great fan of practical jokes, especially if it involved a customer making a purchase.

"Mr. Tweezer, this may all be very funny to you, but it ain't to me. I am trying to run a business here, not a joke shop," he said.

"It's not a joke. This creature is one of the deadliest beings in the world," explained Ebenezer.

The bird-keeper shrugged and went to the back to fetch another cage. He decided that there was no point in complaining if a customer wanted to make such a useless purchase.

Ebenezer looked at the teeny-tiny beast. He still felt afraid of it.

"What's the matter?" asked Bethany.

"I'm thinking about what's going to happen when I run out of potion," he said. "I know I'm going to be tempted to fatten the beast up again."

"We have enough to last you at least eighty years. I think it'll be fine."

"But eighty years go by so fast when you are 512!"

"You're just going to try and make the most of every one. We'll have to start doing things on *your* bucket list as well as mine," she said. "And I'll be there to help you stay good. No more feeding the beast, while I'm around."

Ebenezer smiled and so did Bethany. Neither of them really knew what it took to be good, but both of them were determined to help each other become better people.

The moment was interrupted by the beast biting into Bethany's finger.

"Ow!" she yelled, dropping the beast to the floor. "I'm bleeding!"

"Oof, that does look a bit nasty," said Ebenezer.

The beast grew, so that it was now the size of an even larger worm. The bird-keeper returned from the back of the shop, carrying a metal box, pierced with air holes, which was no bigger than a matchbox.

"Do you have a small bandage?" asked Ebenezer.

"This ain't a pharmacy, it's a bird shop! How many bleedin' times do I have to tell you?!" asked the bird-keeper.

Bethany removed a thousand-pound note from her rucksack and wrapped it around her finger to stop the bleeding. The bird-keeper's eyes widened.

Ebenezer picked the beast up by one of its feet and placed it on the counter. He took a long hard stare at the matchbox cage and wondered whether it was strong enough.

"And this is definitely the best you've got?" asked Ebenezer.

"For the size you're looking for, yeah. And it's definitely strong enough to hold a worm," answered the bird-keeper.

"It's not a worm. It's one of the deadliest creatures in the universe!"

"Well, it's strong enough to hold one of those, too."

The beautiful song came to an end. Claudette flew to greet her listeners. Like all Wintlorian purple-breasted parrots, she was exceptionally well-mannered.

"How do you do?" she said, offering wingshakes to both Bethany and Ebenezer. "I do hope my singing didn't bother you."

"Are you kidding? That was awesome!" enthused Bethany.

"You're too kind," said Claudette. "I only wish that I could sing it for a happier occasion. It's for my recently deceased cousin, you see."

"Oh, I'm sorry," said Ebenezer.

"Don't be. It's not your fault he's dead," said Claudette.

"It is, actually," admitted Ebenezer. "He died while in my care. I wasn't what you would call a model owner. I really am . . . I'm just so sorry."

Purple tears filled Claudette's eyes. She brushed them away with one of her wings.

"It was dashed brave to tell me the truth," she said, tapping Ebenezer on the shoulder. "Thank you."

"Please don't thank me. It makes me feel even worse."

"No one is perfect, and everyone has to die. Be sorry for the mistakes you make and remember the friends who are lost—but don't do any more. It's a downright waste of life to spend too much time living in the past. Patrick wouldn't want that."

"But—"

"Whatever you did, I forgive you. If you want to honor Patrick's memory, then you can do it by bringing some joy into the world."

It was the most moving speech any of them had ever heard from a bird.

"Can I ask you a question?" asked Bethany. She didn't wait for an answer. "If you're so sad about Patrick's death, why did you sing such a happy song?"

"Because it's a song about Patrick's life, not his death. And his life was a very happy one."

Ebenezer thought about what the song of his life would sound like. It would certainly be very long, but there was no guarantee that it would be a happy or an interesting one. He vowed to try and change this, by living the next eighty years of his life in a far more interesting manner.

"Have you any plans for the afternoon?" asked Claudette. "If not, I would love to sing you a few more songs from Patrick's life. There's a particularly amusing tale from the time he went on tour as the warm-up act for ABBA, if you'd like to hear it."

Ebenezer and Bethany were staying at the orphanage while their ceilings were being rebuilt, and while a replacement was being sent for Miss Fizzlewick. They had made plans to celebrate Ebenezer's birthday by holding a grand luncheon with all the children, but Claudette's proposal sounded far more interesting.

"What a marvelous idea," said Ebenezer. "Why don't you come back to the orphanage with us? You'll have a much larger audience for your singing."

"Yeah, and my friend Geoffrey is obsessed with talking parrots!" added Bethany enthusiastically.

"How wonderful! Let's head there right—"

Claudette was interrupted by her own round stomach. It made a sort of whining sound.

"Is that the beginning of the song?" asked Ebenezer.

"No, it's the beginning of hunger," answered Claudette. Then to the bird-keeper, "I don't suppose you have a snack or some morsel of something I could nibble on?"

"No, I don't suppose I do!" said the bird-keeper. He had paid good money for his selection of bird feed, and he had no intention of handing it out for free.

By this point, Bethany's hand had stopped bleeding. She unrolled the bloody thousand-pound note from her finger, and offered it up to the bird-keeper.

"Will this be enough to get her some food?" she asked.

"B-B-Blimey, yes!" spluttered the bird-keeper.

"Excellent," said Claudette. "I'll start with the snack on the counter."

Claudette swooped down and gobbled the beast with one bite. She pulled a funny face afterward.

"That's the strangest worm I've ever eaten," she said. "Why did it taste like boiled cabbage?"

"It wasn't a worm," said Bethany, starting to laugh.

"No, it wasn't," said Ebenezer, bursting into a fit of giggles with her. "That was the deadliest creature in the universe."

THE END . . . ISH

(by that I mean there's more on the next page)

The Beast and the Bird-Keeper

Three weeks later, Bethany and Ebenezer helped the bird-keeper carry the baby grand piano into his shop. Sweat poured off their brows, and their arms ached from the carrying.

"Put it by the counter. I want to be able to play for the customers when they come in," said the bird-keeper. The bird-keeper had bought the instrument and a few other things in a yard sale that Bethany and Ebenezer had held to raise funds for the orphanage. All the items on offer had originally been vomited out by the beast, and the bird-keeper had bought the baby grand from Bethany at the very reasonable (and slightly ridiculous) price of twenty worms.

"Do you need help with anything else?" asked Ebenezer.

"We don't have any time, you nitwit. We need to go," said Bethany.

"If you need any help feeding the birds, or clearing out their cages, or even just talking to them in soothing tones—just let us know. We'd be happy to stick around to help you out," said Ebenezer to the bird-keeper.

"We'll be happy to do no such thing!" said Bethany.

She had a day of do-gooding planned for the two of them. Ebenezer was far from excited.

"There's nothing you can help me with, I'm afraid, Mr. Tweezer. You'd probably get it all wrong anyway," said the bird-keeper. "But I don't see why on earth you're getting involved with all this do-gooding nonsense. Sounds like nothing but a waste of energy to me."

"Exactly, it's a waste of time, too! I've only got eighty years left to live, now that the beast is gone," said Ebenezer, brimming with self-pity.

"We've been through this already. Eighty years is flipping loads, and we're gonna make sure we live those years in a better way. Get in the car. I'm not arguing with you about this anymore," said Bethany.

She dragged Ebenezer out of the shop and into the

car. The bird-keeper was left with nothing but his birds for company.

He took a seat at his brand-new piano. He hoped that his new purchase would help attract customers and bring joy to the birds.

Unfortunately, the piano did neither of these things.

The bird-keeper was not a natural musician, and he had refused to take lessons because he thought it was a waste of money. The sounds he made on the piano over the following day were far from pleasant, and so his playing not only drove customers away from the shop, but also angered the birds.

As he sat that evening, trying, and failing, to play "Pop Goes the Weasel," the birds finally made their feelings of anger clear by clucking, shrieking, hooting, tweeting, and quacking at him in an aggressive manner.

"Oh, shut up!" he shouted back at them. "I'd like to hear you lot try to play 'Pop Goes the Weasel.' It ain't half a hard song to master!"

The birds responded by singing, in beautiful harmony, the entirety of the song. They were about to launch into an encore, but they were silenced when the bird-keeper threatened to stop feeding them.

"And if I hear so much as one more chirp out of any of you, I'll send you all to the rescued cats' home," he added.

He listened carefully for a good ten seconds and was happy to find that his threat had worked. He cracked his knuckles, stretched his fingers, and was about to resume playing his unusual version of the song, when he was interrupted by another bird. This time, however, it was not one of his own.

Claudette, the Wintlorian purple-breasted parrot, was knocking her beak at the window of the shop. The bird-keeper sighed and opened the door. He was about to tell her to get lost, but then he noticed that the past three weeks had not been kind to her. She had lost a lot of weight, and her sparkling blue eyes were bloodshot with sleeplessness.

"What's the matter with you?" he asked, as he beckoned her in.

"I haven't the foggiest!" she said. "But I've been feeling just dreadful ever since I ate that strange cabbagey creature. Are Ebenezer and Bethany around? I need to ask them some questions about it."

"No, they're off do-gooding," replied the bird-keeper.

"Oh blast. I'm giving a concert tonight, and I was hoping to see them before then," said Claudette.

The bird-keeper could see she was upset, and he took pity on her. He had never been able to refuse a bird who needed his help.

"Do you want me to run some tests?" he offered. "I should be able to tell you what's wrong with you in about half an hour or so."

But after about a half an hour or so, and a series of X-rays, blood tests, and claw and beak inspections, the bird-keeper couldn't find anything that needed fixing.

"How odd," said the bird-keeper. "All the tests are saying that you are an incredibly healthy parrot."

"But I don't feel healthy," said Claudette.

"What *do* you feel?"

"I feel . . . *hungry*. And I don't understand it, because I've been eating such a lot of food."

The bird-keeper looked at Claudette's belly. She certainly didn't look like someone who had eaten a lot of food. He looked back up to her face. For a brief moment, he could have sworn that one of her sparkling blue eyes had turned black.

"I think you're gonna have to speak to Ebenezer and Bethany about this. Maybe they can tell you something about the creature you ate that I don't know," he said.

"I'll have to hunt them down, and get them to join me backstage at the concert," said Claudette, in a strange voice. An unfriendly look came into her eyes. "I can't wait to see Bethany again."

"Is everything okay?"

Claudette shook her head, and the strange voice and unfriendly look disappeared. "Sorry about that, I felt a bit peculiar for a moment. But yes, anyway, I must go. Thank you ever so much for your help."

The bird-keeper led Claudette back to the front door and held it open for her. She flew away, her purple body disappearing into the night sky. But while the door was still open, something strange happened.

The piano started playing a tune of its own. The song was far more horrid than "Pop Goes the Weasel."

Read on for a taste of
Revenge of the Beast.

The Beastly Beginning

When Ebenezer Tweezer was eleven years old, the world was much younger.

Instead of cars on the streets, there were horses and carriages. In place of phones and computers, people would communicate via letters and hopeful shouting.

There was no such thing as photographs, and so if you were the sort of person who liked to capture the moment whenever you happened to be wearing a nice outfit or eating a pretty meal, you would have to travel around with your own personal portrait artist. Electricity was nothing more than a silly word back then, which meant that you could only read books past bedtime if you had an extensive collection of candles.

In short, it was a pretty rotten time to be alive. And for poor Ebenezer, it was especially rotten, because he was a deeply unpopular child.

It's hard to say exactly what made him so unpopular. Perhaps it was because he had a smug-looking face, or it might have had something to do with the fact that his outfits were always rather extravagant—filled with ruffles and colorful patterns.

Whatever the reason, it was clear that the other children did not care for young Ebenezer. He was never invited to their feasts, jester jousts, or theater trips, but this didn't deter him from arriving uninvited. In fact, Ebenezer would spend most afternoons lurking outside the Muddlington Pie Shoppe because he knew that, from time to time, the children would gather there and challenge each other to impromptu pasty-eating competitions.

More often than not, though, Ebenezer would spend entire days outside the pie shop, and no children would arrive. Ebenezer would use the time to practice his conversation skills by talking to the wall. He'd say things like:

"Isn't it a fine day we're having?"

Or:

"Have you seen that new comedy by Willy Whatshis-name? No, I didn't get any of the jokes either."

And:

"Such a rotter about that plague, isn't it?"

Invariably, the wall didn't have anything to say. But Ebenezer didn't mind, because he saw all these one-sided chats as terribly good warm-ups for the real thing. He was sure that if he could only strike upon the right topic of conversation, or wear the right number of ruffles on his shirt, then the other children would let him join in with their pasty-filled merriment.

On one such day, when he was lurking outside the pie shop, Ebenezer became aware of a commotion taking place in the square. The town crier had given up his usual shouting about the wonderful deals available at his wife's haberdashery and was now crying something in an urgent voice. Ebenezer wasn't able to hear the exact words because the commotion and uproar in the street was too loud.

Serious-looking men, wearing some very silly scarlet capes and green stockings, were dismounting from their horses. They each carried a trumpet in their hand, as if it were a weapon, and their faces were grave with worry.

"You there, boy!" shouted one of them. Ebenezer saw there was a crest on the capes, which read DIVISION OF

REMOVING RAPSCALLIONS IN SECRET. "Have you seen the deadliest creature that has ever tormented this earth?"

Ebenezer was pretty sure that he would have remembered such a creature, but he was a well-behaved child, and he wanted to be as helpful as possible. It took him about twelve seconds to flick through his memories.

"No, I'm almost certain I haven't," said Ebenezer. "Is this a game of hide-and-seek? No one's agreed to play it with me yet, but I don't think you're meant to ask for help."

"This is no game, boy! If we don't capture the creature before it regains its strength, there's no telling what might happen," said the cape-wearer.

"Oh, deary me," said Ebenezer. "I wish I could help. But like I said, no creatures have crossed my path. Sorry."

The cape-wearer seemed to take this remark as a personal insult. He huffily returned to his horse and trotted away from Ebenezer. The rest of the cape-and-stocking wearers continued their search—bursting into establishments and asking pointed questions—but Ebenezer's attention was soon drawn elsewhere when he spotted three children approaching the pie shop.

"I hear they caught it in Lady Morgana's basement. Apparently she'd been keeping it hidden from the Division for centuries," said Nicholas Nickle, an unpleasant boy with a suitably unpleasant face.

"No one lives for centuries, so that's clearly not true, brother dearest," said Nicholas's distinctly undear sister, Nicola Nickle. "I heard that the creature used to be the size of a small hill, until the Division fed it a trumpet. One of Morgana's neighbors said they saw the creature deflating like a balloon and whooshing out of the house."

"I WANT SOME STOCKINGS!" said Nicco Nickle, the youngest child of the ghastly family.

The Nickles were generally viewed by the rest of the neighborhood as menaces, but Ebenezer was not in a position to be fussy about friends. As they approached, Ebenezer tousled the ruffles on his shirt and tried to remember his small-talk training.

"Isn't it a rotter about this Willy comedy, eh? No, I didn't get the plague at all," said Ebenezer. A frown wrinkled his brow. "Hang on a moment. I think I might have gotten that a bit up-jumbled."

The Nickles' faces lit up. Ebenezer mistook this as an expression of friendship, so his face lit up too.

"Well, well, well—look who's here for another beating. It's only Mr. Ebenoozer Loooooseerrrr," said Nicholas.

"I love it when you call me that," said Ebenezer, deadly serious. "I read somewhere that it's very important for friends to have nicknames for one another."

"We're not your friends, Ebenooozer. I thought we showed you last time what happens when you call us that," said Nicholas.

"Hmm? Oh yes, that game where you chase me whilst throwing sticks and stones is great fun," said Ebenezer. "But perhaps this time we could just have a little chat instead? The wall and I have been practicing for hours."

However, it soon became clear that the Nickles were not in the mood for a spot of sparkling conversation. The three of them charged at Ebenezer, chasing him through the square and out onto the fields that led to the back of his house. They hurled names, insults, and the occasional rock at the back of his head.

Ebenezer was comfortably able to outrun them because he was blessed with a pair of long, gangly legs. As he ran, he tried to convince himself that this was just another game, even though he knew, deep down, that it wasn't. Like everyone else, the Nickles had taken an immediate dislike to Ebenezer, and he was powerless to do anything about it.

There was no amount of shirt-shopping or wall-talking that was going to make them like or respect him.

But then, as he was sprinting through the final field, he stepped on something squishy. He looked under his shoe and found that the squishy something was a worm-sized blob of gray. As he peered even closer, he was able to make out three black eyes, two black tongues, and a dribbling mouth. It had a set of tiny limbs, and its breath stank of boiled cabbage.

"*Help me,*" said the squishy something as he scraped it off his shoe.

Ebenezer was so shocked by the voice that he dropped the squishy something. He quickly picked it back up and dusted away the specks of mud from its eyes.

"Terribly sorry about that," he said. As he looked at the squishy something, he knew he was holding something extraordinary. For a few seconds, he just stood gazing at it, but then he remembered his manners. "My name's Ebenoo—I mean, Ebenezer."

"And I am a beast. Please, you're my only hope—help me."

The De-Beasting

W hat a creature—so unlike anything I've ever seen!
Such beauty, such poise, such grace—you deserve the
world, and I'm going to jolly well make sure I give it to you."

Five hundred years later, Ebenezer was soaking in his
morning bubble bath, whispering sweet nothings to the
reflection in his handheld mirror. Over the centuries, he
had learned that mirrors are much easier to talk to than
walls—especially when you have a rigorous potion-and-
skin-care routine that gives you a face as beautiful as a
twilight moon.

"Why the sad face?" Ebenezer asked himself. "The
morning bath has always been a happy occasion!"

Over the course of his long, long lifetime, Ebenezer had
soaked in almost two hundred thousand baths, and they

had all been very happy occasions indeed. Today, however, there was something amok.

For one thing, Ebenezer's windup rubber ducky was missing. This was a serious blow to proceedings, because Raphael was a ducky who had performed tricks and sung moving sea shanties every morning since the beast had vomited him out.

For another, there was something peculiar about the smell in the room. Thanks to the beast, Ebenezer was accustomed to baths that were bubbled and salted with only the very finest products a man can bathe in, and yet there was a distinctly cheap and nasty odor leaking out of the bubbles—as if someone had replaced his salts with dishwasher powder.

For the third, final, and most-disturbing-of-all thing, there was a smudgy, greasy-fingered message from Bethany on his handheld mirror:

OI, GITFACE. NO TIME FOR BATHING TODAY. DE-BEASTING TO BE DONE.

Naturally, Ebenezer had ignored the message, because it was his long-held belief that there is always time for a bath. He believed that you often need to take a bath right at the moment when other people would have you believe that there is no time for one.

However, the message continued to vex and irk because it made him wonder what Bethany had planned for their day, and eventually his curiosity could take it no more. He cut his bath short by a couple of hours; threw on some loungewear, slippers, and a dressing gown; and made his way downstairs.

His journey was fraught with confusion and peril because certain items in the fifteen-story house seemed to have gone walkabout. Confusion clouded his face when he noticed that all the furnishings from the velvet suite had been replaced with deck chairs and whoopee cushions. The confusion gave way to alarm when he found that his favorite collection of beautiful paintings had been taken off the wall. In their place was a selection of doodles and unconvincingly proportioned stick figures, which had been graffitied onto the wallpaper and signed by Bethany.

"No, no, no!" said Ebenezer, sprinting downstairs to address Bethany in his best *I'm really rather cross with you* sort of voice. "What on earth are you doing?"

"Stupid question," said Bethany. She was quite right,

because it was perfectly obvious that she was trying to remove a piano from the front room of the house. "Gimme a hand, gitface. We've gotta get this onto the street with the other stuff."

"I shall do no such thing!" said Ebenezer. "I'm not going to help you rob me."

"We're not robbing you; we're helping you. Claudette and I have been working our flipping butts off," said Bethany.

And then, as if to show off her butt-working, Claudette the Wintlorian purple-breasted parrot flew into the house. Her feathery forehead was slightly damp with sweat.

"That's the last of the dancing teapots done, poppets!" she said, spreading her wings in a *Ta-da!* pose. "Hi-de-hi, Ebenezer! Has Bethany told you about our wonderful de-beasting mission?"

"De-beasting?" asked Ebenezer.

"Yeah," said Bethany matter-of-factly. "De-beasting."

Claudette sank her talons into the piano and assisted Bethany in her efforts to drag it out of the room. They were neither strong enough nor strategic enough to move the instrument without causing great damage to the walls and floors.

"Why do we need to de-beast?" he asked. "Claudette *killed* the beast; I'd say that's a pretty thorough de-beasting already."

"How very dare you—I'm not a killer! I just happened to accidentally eat it, and I've been feeling simply awful ever since," said Claudette, puffing her feathery belly.

"Don't feel awful. The beast was a wicked, terrible monster who tried to eat me!" said Bethany.

"Oh yes, I know that, but you've somewhat misunderstood me. I really have been *feeling* awful. Indigestion, or something like that. I haven't had a good night's sleep in weeks," said Claudette.

"Still not seeing what any of this has to do with you two pinching all my things," said Ebenezer.

"It's not *all* your things; it's just the stuff the beast vomited out for you. Claudette said it would be good for us," said Bethany. "I don't want to look at all the stuff, and neither should you. Like this piano—do you remember who you fed the beast to get it?"

Ebenezer looked at his slippers with a shameful expression upon his face. In order to get the piano, he had fed the beast Patrick—another Wintlorian purple-breasted parrot, who happened to be a cousin of Claudette's. Claudette had been remarkably forgiving about the whole thing.

"All right, we can sell the piano and maybe some of the gold-plated cutlery," said Ebenezer. He reluctantly joined in with the piano-moving operation as they squeezed it through the front door. "But we mustn't go too crazy with it."

Once they got outside, Ebenezer realized they had already gone far too crazy. The lawn was covered with various gifts that the beast had vomited out for him over the past five centuries—all the things Ebenezer had asked for at the beginning, which he thought might help him make friends, and all the other stuff in the centuries that followed, which he got just for himself, or to make other people jealous.

Ebenezer's bath salts were there, and so was Raphael—the windup rubber ducky. There were dessert fridges, self-decorating Christmas trees, a mind-reading vacuum cleaner that tidies rooms whenever you think they look a bit dusty, televisions the size of bedsheets, an astronaut suit—and many other strange and wonderful things. Ebenezer felt as if his whole life with the beast was on display for the world to see.

Looking for another great book?
Find it
IN THE MIDDLE.

Fun, fantastic books for kids
in the in-be**TWEEN** age.

IntheMiddleBooks.com

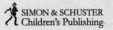

READ & LEARN

with

simon kids

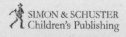
75458